BLOODSTAINED
DIAMONDS
The Fall

Torunn Agtind

Foreword

Russia has always drawn me with its contradictions—a land of immeasurable wealth and unbearable poverty, of dazzling beauty and ruthless violence. It is a country forged in revolution, scarred by the collapse of empires, and reborn again and again through fire. The Russia of 2005 still bore the ghosts of communism's fall, its people struggling to navigate the chaos of a world reshaped by ambition, greed, and survival.

Within this fragile landscape walks Viktor—a man ground down by the monotony of factory life in Novgorod, yet restless for something more. His yearning collides with Boris Jumashyev, a Moscow oligarch whose hunger for power knows no limits. What follows is not merely the pursuit of diamonds, but a descent into the shadowed heart of post-Soviet Russia—where money buys loyalty, betrayal cuts deep, and love becomes as dangerous as violence.

This is a story of ambition and survival, of choices that carve destinies in blood. *Bloodstained Diamonds – The Fall* is not just about riches unearthed from the earth, but the human cost buried beneath them.

Acknowledgements

I would like to express my deepest gratitude to Blake Edward and Ashley Ross at BookFuel, whose patience, dedication, and thorough attention to detail have greatly contributed to improving the manuscript. Their insightful suggestions for revisions and enhancements have been invaluable throughout the process.

Dedication

I would also like to extend my heartfelt gratitude to my brother Erik and my partner Otto, for their unwavering support and boundless patience as I worked on writing this series.

Disclaimer

Any resemblance to real persons, living or deceased, is entirely coincidental.

Contents

Prologue

The military trucks screeched to a halt outside the grand palace entrance, their engines growling like restless beasts. Peasant soldiers, clad in threadbare uniforms patched with red armbands bearing crude black letters, leapt down from the truck beds. Their heavy boots struck the frozen ground with deliberate thuds. A sharp command shattered the icy morning air, followed by the relentless pounding of boots echoing through the opulent marble halls.

"They're here!" a terrified voice cried, slicing through the tense stillness. The duke and duchess snapped into frantic motion, herding their children up the marble staircase. Their hurried footsteps blended with the sounds of the soldiers' advance below. Slamming the bedroom door shut, they pressed their trembling bodies against it. Desperation was etched into every line of their faces.

"We should have left sooner," the duchess whispered, her voice barely steady.

"And gone where?" the duke shot back, his fear breaking through his usual composure. "They would have hunted us down no matter where we ran." For months, they had lived under the constant shadow of revolution. Each day brought more uncertainty, more peril. But the dread they now faced eclipsed all that had come before. The duke's haggard face, his sunken eyes haunted by sleepless nights, revealed a man pushed beyond his limits. His hands trembled as he gripped his hunting rifle — a desperate lifeline and a futile gesture against the gathering storm.

The duchess sat rigid on the edge of the bed, her daughters clutching her on either side. The elder child gripped her mother's hand so tightly her knuckles whitened, her pale face drawn tight with fear.

"Are we going to die?" her voice was barely more than a breath.

"No, darling," the duchess replied quickly, brushing a comforting finger over her daughter's cheek. "Your papa won't let anything happen to us."

The younger girl whimpered softly, golden curls trembling as her mother's fingers stroked them, a futile balm against the growing dread.

"Hush, my love," the duchess murmured, her own voice betraying the fear she tried to hide. "It's going to be all right."

The thunder of boots climbed the marble staircase, each step measured and unyielding. The soldiers drew closer.

Suddenly, the door burst open with a deafening crash. Duke Nikolai Nikolayevich sprang to his feet, rifle raised and voice sharp as ice. "What do you want here? Speak!"

The soldiers froze, faces etched with irritation and hesitation as they stared down the gun pointed directly at them.

"We've come to take what's ours!" snarled a young soldier, stepping forward with a defiant sneer.

Nikolai's gaze locked onto the youth, eyes narrowing in a cold mix of recognition and contempt. "You," he spat. "You're the son of one of my serfs. This land, this palace —

it belongs to me. Leave now, peasant, before you disgrace yourself."

The young soldier's eyes blazed. He tightened his grip on the rifle slung across his chest. "We come in Lenin's name!" he roared, pride and fury shaking his voice. "And we stop for no one!"

"Don't argue with him!" hissed another soldier, unease flickering across his face.

Outside, a swelling crowd roared their fury, voices rising into a frenzied chant: "Down with the capitalists! All land to the people! Mother Russia's riches are ours!"

The duke's chest tightened as he took in the defiant boy — once a frightened serf's son, now a man wielding a rifle and vengeance in his heart. His gaze flicked to his family: a trembling wife, terrified daughters pressed close.

"We can't fight them," the duchess whispered, voice fragile, eyes glistening with tears. "Please, Nikolai. For the children."

He understood the cost of resistance — blood, suffering far beyond their means to bear. His hands trembled as he lowered the rifle, the weapon clattering hollowly to the floor. Slowly, he sank back onto the bed, pulling his family close as if his embrace alone could shield them from the storm raging now within their once-safe home.

The soldiers swarmed in, the air thick with acrid sweat, unwashed uniforms, and the raw scent of fear.

"Sit still!" barked the young soldier with cruel authority.

The family froze, helpless, as the looting began. Silverware clinked, fine china shattered, and ornate treasures disappeared into rough burlap sacks. Priceless paintings were torn from walls. Hidden jewels, secreted away by the duchess, were wrested from their resting places and thrust into filthy hands.

One soldier stuffed a diamond necklace deep into his pocket as the duchess's voice, barely a whisper, broke through the chaos. "Please… it belonged to my deceased mother."

Her plea hung desperate in the thick air.

The young soldier sneered. "So what? You'll have nothing left," he hissed, venom dripping from every syllable.

The duke clenched his fists, heart pounding with helpless rage. Nearby, the duchess murmured hollow reassurances to her daughters, her own faith crumbling as the last remnants of their world vanished into the cold.

Chapter 1

She stumbled along the sidewalk beside the Neva River, her chest heavy and eyes burning, terrified for her life. Each step was hurried, almost frantic, her gaze locked on the restless waters swirling beside the wide avenue. The sun warmed her cheeks, but it was a distant comfort, barely registering against the storm of fear and sorrow that gripped her. For nearly an hour, she had wandered, lost in a current of dread, her mind racing while the river's steady flow mirrored the chaos within—a life unraveling, slipping from her grasp like sunlight on moving water.

What could she do now? How could she survive this?

Ahead, the Winter Palace rose like a silent sentinel beneath the hazy glow of the early hour, its regal silhouette above the glittering waters of the Neva. The palace's grandeur radiated in soft golds and faded greens, its beauty distant and unfeeling—completely indifferent to the turmoil churning inside her. Cars zipped past on the road next to the sidewalk in both directions, their headlights flaring and windows flashing like accusations—accusatory glances slicing through the quiet street with a sharp, judging glare. Nearby, a docked restaurant boat rested against the quay, its deck aglow with soft lights, adorned with fluttering banners and glowing lanterns, alive with the clinking of glasses and bursts of laughter. Through the veil of her tears, she barely registered the diners' carefree joy—a stark contrast to the shadows edging ever closer to her own.

A commotion pulled her attention forward.

Just ahead, in a park by the water, a man barked harsh commands at a bear cub. Its snout was cruelly taped shut, silencing its whimpers as it stumbled weakly across the grass, tugged this way and that. The man's grip tightened around its neck and yanked without mercy. With a grunt of effort, he hoisted it high, brandishing it like a grotesque trophy to a group of stunned American tourists, their expressions locked in polite horror. The bear's pitiful, muffled cry pierced the air—the helpless flailing of its tiny paws twisted something raw inside her, aching and unforgettable. It cut through her like a blade, tearing open a wound she thought she had buried.

A hot wave of rage surged through her, scorching away the numbness. The cruelty. The callousness. It was too much.

"You devil!" she screamed, her voice hoarse and trembling, a cry torn from the depths of her grief. "A devil!"

A few heads turned. Eyes flicked toward her, full of fleeting curiosity, then just as quickly away. The man didn't flinch. The tourists shifted uncomfortably, some lifting phones, others looking down—their inaction as sharp as the man's cruelty. The rage within her boiled over into despair—a bitter, familiar feeling twisting in her chest. Tears rolled down her cheeks and she let them fall, unashamed. The world went on, dazzling and indifferent, unmoved by the suffering clinging to her like heat in stagnant air.

"You devil!" she shrieked again, her voice raw and trembling with rage so potent it startled even her. "A devil!"

Heads turned briefly—only for a moment—then her desperate cry was swallowed by the hum of a vibrant early morning. The man, a hulking shadow against the hazy light of the avenue, didn't flinch. The tourists recoiled but did nothing, at first uneasy, then returning their phones to idle, discomfort fading into passive observation.

Fury surged through her—hot and impotent—and she stumbled forward, tears streaming freely now, a scalding, helpless wave leaving her shaking. It was the familiar ache of injustice. Of being unseen. Of witnessing cruelty in a world too distracted by its own comfort to care. The tears weren't just grief—they were the embodiment of the storm roaring inside her.

To her right, the Winter Palace rose in all its baroque splendor, its ornate golden trims gleaming brightly against the soft blue sky. But its majesty felt like a taunt—a relic of a time and power that no longer existed in any form that served justice. The Hermitage Museum, renowned worldwide for its treasures and art collections, felt hollow— an echo of a world long gone—disconnected from the harsh realities surrounding her. It was beautiful. But it meant nothing.

Her legs trembled, her feet stiff from aimless wandering along the wide avenues and sidewalks under the dim early light. Her throat was dry, her limbs heavy with fatigue and grief—but in the haze, a sharp focus snapped into place. The fog of uncertainty lifted.

She had a destination now—a friend's.

A friend – who answered her desperate call for help. An apartment nearby—a sanctuary where she could lay low away from watchful eyes, not far from here. A modest refuge tucked behind a peeling iron gate and a courtyard blooming with forgotten roses. It wasn't much. But it was all she had.

She gripped her worn leather bag tighter, the strap sticky against her damp palm. Pressed urgently into her side was a flash drive—a sliver of plastic and metal holding the weight of the truth. Evidence that Boris Jumashyev, the oligarch ruling with unchecked greed, was guilty of vast corruption and crime. That proof had cost her American journalist boyfriend, Paul, his life.

Paul had died for this.

The thought struck her like a thunderclap. His name rang through her chest, echoing with all they had sacrificed. The memory was as vivid as the morning light the day he was shot.

He had trusted her with this.

And now, the burden—and the danger—was hers alone.

This early morning unfolded in agonizing detail: *they had left their apartment together, sunlight spilling in through gauzy curtains. The air was thick with the scent of blooming jasmine from the window box. Paul stepped outside first, his familiar smile warming her even in that quiet early hour—a presence grounding her in a world teetering on the edge.*

Even as she fumbled with her keys—her fingers unsteady— he waited, calm and reassuring, bathed in the soft morning light. For one brief moment, everything felt bearably normal. He looked so alive—so present—as though nothing could shatter the illusion of safety.

[15]

She had barely noticed the motorcycle idling at the curb, its rider cloaked in black riding gear, helmet reflecting the pale light. The engine growled low, like a predator biding its time.

Then came the sharp crack of a shotgun. A sound that split the morning air like a lightning strike.

Paul's smile vanished in an instant. His eyes widened more in disbelief than pain, as his body jerked violently and crumpled to the sunlit pavement.

The world reeled, but her body acted on instinct—dropping to her knees beside him before her mind could catch up.

"Paul!" she cried, voice breaking with disbelief. Her hands trembled as she grasped his arm, pleading through tears. "Get up! Please, please, get up!"

But it was no use. His breath came shallow and uneven. Blood seeped across his chest, staining his shirt and pooling beneath him—a vivid blot against the concrete. The scene was a nightmare she couldn't escape.

Then—another shot.

Glass exploded somewhere nearby. Shards rained down, catching the light like deadly confetti. Pain lanced across her temple and she stumbled backward, one hand flying to her bleeding head. The warmth of her blood against her skin was disorienting.

The motorcycle's engine rumbled low like a predator poised to strike. Its rider, cloaked in black armor, sat unnervingly still—helmet visor a void of impenetrable darkness. The menace radiated silent and absolute—like death incarnate in the quiet morning.

In that suspended moment, the chaos of her world crystallized with brutal clarity: Paul was gone. And now—they wanted her.

The realization struck like a thunderclap, knocking the wind from her lungs. The rider hadn't been waiting just for someone. He was waiting for them.

Paul was undeniably, tragically dead. And now, she was the target.

Panic surged—a primal, electric wave. She slammed the door of the apartment building behind her and yanked it shut just as bullets tore through the thin wood, splinters flying like angry hornets. Every crack of gunfire was a blow to her fractured reality.

She bolted up the narrow staircase, feet pounding a frantic rhythm. Sweat slicked her brow, lungs searing with fear. Then, as abruptly as it started, the gunfire stopped.

A door above creaked open, a sliver of warm light spilling into the stairwell. A man's hand reached out and grabbed her arm, pulling her inside the safety of his apartment. She collapsed just inside the door, breath ragged, skin damp with sweat and blood, crouching by the open window, daring to peer over the sill.

The street below was unnaturally still. The space where the motorcycle had stood was now empty. The tension that had hung thick moments ago was gone, replaced by a cruel calm.

"They're gone," the man muttered beside her, voice low and firm. "Stay here—it's not safe."

But she pulled away, resolve hardening like steel. A sudden, searing focus cleared the fog of fear. She had to go back.

Without hesitation, she darted from the apartment, sprinting downstairs, each step pounding a drumbeat of defiance. Her heart thundered in her ears, louder than her hurried footsteps.

Paul lay where she left him—still on the pavement, his body casting a long, motionless shadow in the pale light. The sight sent fresh anguish crashing through her. She dropped to her knees beside him, hands trembling as she searched for a pulse. There was none.

"No…" she whispered, voice breaking into sobs. Hot tears streamed down her cheeks. She pressed a trembling kiss to his forehead, lips brushing the stillness of his skin. The silence screamed the truth she couldn't bear.

In the distance, the wailing sirens of police cars grew louder, piercing the early morning air.

But she didn't trust the police—not after all she had seen of their corruption and indifference.

She couldn't risk staying.

Her soul screamed against it, needing more time just to hold onto him.

Staggering upright, legs trembling under grief's weight, she turned for one last look, committing his face to memory— even as tears blurred her vision.

*Then, chest heavy and eyes burning, she turned and ran—
into the heat, into the noise, into whatever waited for her
next.*

Her breath caught painfully in her throat as she neared the
intersection by the Dvortsovy Bridge. The golden summer
sun dipped low on the horizon, casting long, amber shadows
across the cobbled streets. And then she saw it—a dark shape
roaring toward her through the shimmering heatwaves, the
growl of its engine rising like thunder. The motorcycle.
Black-clad. Menacing. Unstoppable.

Her chest constricted; her heartbeat stuttered. It was him.
The killer. The shadow she had tried so desperately to
outrun.

For a single, suspended moment, the city fell into a strange
hush. The usual hum of traffic, laughter from a riverside
café, the clink of cutlery—all faded, muffled beneath the
weight of dread. She stood frozen, limbs locked in fear, her
body refusing to move even as danger closed in like a storm.

Then, like a lightning strike, instinct shattered the paralysis.
Her legs kicked into motion, pounding against the sun-
warmed pavement. Every breath scorched her lungs, every
muscle screamed in protest, but adrenaline drove her
forward. She sprinted toward the quay, where sleek
hydrofoil boats bobbed gently at their moorings—silent
sentinels of hope on the glinting river.

The nearest boat rose before her, brilliant in the first light of
day. Its gangway jutted out like a tightrope to freedom. She
launched herself toward it, feet thudding against the narrow
metal walkway, slick with spilled drinks and faint traces of

sunscreen. The morning sun glinted off the metal, warming her soles, but she barely noticed, heart hammering like a drum inside her chest.

Then came the crack—sharp and terrible. A gunshot tore through the warm air.

Agony burst at the base of her skull, a blinding jolt that dropped her instantly. Her vision fractured like shattered glass as she collapsed against the gangway's metal surface, her body jerking once, then going limp.

Her leather bag slipped from her shoulder. The strap slithered down her arm like a snake and tumbled over the edge into the water below. The river, golden with sunlight and deceptively calm, swallowed it whole—along with the flash drive tucked inside. The truth. The evidence. Paul's legacy.

Darkness bled into the corners of her sight, slow and steady at first, then faster—deeper—pulling her into its endless silence. The sun still glimmered above her, its warmth mocking the cold that crept through her limbs. And then it was gone. The light. The warmth. The fight. All of it faded into the quiet embrace of night.

Chapter 2

The sunlight, filtered and fractured by the thick, ancient canopy of trees overhead, scattered like countless flecks of molten gold over the sprawling, manicured estates. Each beam that pierced the emerald gloom seemed to illuminate a secret, hinting at the vast wealth hidden beneath the lush foliage. The midday heat, a heavy, humid blanket, was stifling, pressing down on the very air, broken only by the faint, sporadic, almost desperate barking of a distant dog—a solitary sound swallowed quickly by the oppressive quiet. Otherwise, a profound, almost reverent silence hung heavy over this exclusive suburb of Moscow, a silence purchased at great cost, where the country's newly minted elite, the nouveau riche, engaged in a silent, cutthroat competition to erect and inhabit the grandest, most impregnable palaces. Here, status was measured not just in square footage, but in the sheer audacity of one's architectural statement.

The most opulent among them all, a newly constructed white mansion that boasted two imposing stories crowned by a soaring loft, remained a whispered legend from the sidewalk. Its dazzling facade, a testament to unbridled ambition and imported marble, was barely visible, a tantalizing glimpse for the curious and the envious. Its splendor was almost entirely obscured by a colossal, meticulously crafted stone wall, nearly three meters high, its rough-hewn blocks speaking of both ancient strength and modern exclusion. And guarding the sole, formidable entrance was an iron gate of intricate, almost gothic design, formidable and heavily guarded, ensuring not just privacy, but an impenetrable fortress of wealth, a stark declaration that those within lived in a world utterly separate from the ordinary. The air itself seemed to hum with the unspoken understanding of absolute power and the lengths to which it would go to secure its sanctuary.

Boris Jumashyev sat in his spacious first-floor office, the air thick with the faint scent of leather-bound ledgers and polished wood. His sharp gaze was locked onto a formidable stack of business documents spread across the imposing mahogany desk, each page a testament to deals inked and fortunes amassed. The wide windows were thrown open, inviting a cool draft that stirred the heavy velvet curtains with a slow, deliberate rhythm—yet outside, the air hung unnervingly still, as if the world beyond his walls awaited his next move with bated breath.

The sudden trill of the phone shattered the heavy silence, its piercing sound cutting through the calm like a dagger. Boris's eyes flicked to the glowing screen, his expression tightening momentarily, hardening like steel under pressure. He rose without hesitation, the leather of his chair creaking softly beneath him as he moved to close the open windows, shutting out the stillness and the view of his meticulously maintained estate. The sound of the latch snapping echoed with a finality that seemed to signal the closing off of distractions.

Settling back into his chair, Boris's gaze drifted briefly toward the newly installed swimming pool shimmering under the sun—a crystal oasis of blue nestled amid manicured hedges and marble walkways. The pool, gleaming and pristine, was more than a feature of luxury; it was a symbol of power, wealth, and control, reflecting the man's ambitions as clearly as the polished surfaces before him.

"Yes," he said again into the phone, his voice clipped and commanding. He listened intently to the voice on the other end, words washing over him like currents beneath a calm surface. But beneath Boris's apparent composure, a storm of calculation and cold strategy churned. Every call, every whispered tidbit of information, was a move on a chessboard stretched far beyond his office walls.

Outside, through the glass, the courtyard revealed a contrasting scene of labor and sweat. His private chauffeur, sleeves rolled up against the stifling heat, scrubbed diligently at a sleek black car parked near the detached garage. The man had shed his dark uniform jacket, revealing a crisp white shirt now marred with large patches of sweat seeping under his arms—an unspoken testament to the physical toil supporting the gilded life within the mansion's walls. This juxtaposition—of measured power inside and humble labor outside—was a reminder of the invisible gears that turned the vast machine of Boris Jumashyev's empire.

In that moment, Boris allowed himself a brief, almost imperceptible tightening of his jaw, a flicker of internal conflict. The facade of control was absolute, yet lurking beneath was the ever-present awareness of the cost—the subtle tensions between dominion and vulnerability, between the man and the world he sought to command.

The expected confirmation came through, delivered in clipped, efficient words over the receiver. Boris exhaled slowly, a deliberate release of tension that had coiled tight for days. His lips curled into a faint, almost imperceptible smile—a shadow of satisfaction that settled deep within him as he ended the call with a decisive click.

He crossed the length of the room with measured ease, the polished hardwood floor beneath his feet echoing softly in the quiet space. At the far end, a well-stocked bar gleamed under subdued lighting, an array of crystal decanters and gleaming bottles promising brief respite from the relentless currents of power and intrigue. Boris's hand hovered momentarily before selecting a chilled bottle of vodka, its glass catching glints of light like a rare jewel. He poured himself a generous measure, the clear liquid filling the glass with a reassuring steadiness.

Raising the glass, his gaze drifted once more through the wide windows to the courtyard. The swimming pool's surface glittered, disturbed only by a lazy ripple on the breeze. Boris's eyes lingered on the stillness outside, as if seeking affirmation not just from the scene but from the invisible forces that governed his world.

Thoughts swirled behind those steely eyes, dark and complex—calculations of risk and reward, power moves and unspoken threats. The American journalist, with his relentless probing, and the meddling girlfriend who had tangled herself in matters far beyond her ken, had been dealt with swiftly, their interference extinguished like a candle in a gale. The problem in St. Petersburg was resolved, buried beneath layers of silence and shadow.

He downed the vodka in a single, smooth gulp, the burn of the spirit warming his throat, fueling the grim satisfaction that settled over him like armor. Setting the empty glass down on the polished counter with a muted clink, Boris allowed his smile to deepen, a predator's expression of quiet triumph.

"All taken care of," he murmured under his breath, the words heavy with finality and undisputed authority. Yet beneath that calm exterior, there flickered a subtle edge—an unvoiced awareness that power, while intoxicating, was fragile, always vulnerable to the next unseen challenge lurking just beyond the horizon.

Chapter 3

The sunlight struggled weakly through the sparse crowns of brittle trees that clawed their way skyward from the crumbling outskirts of Novgorod. Here, lines of aging apartment blocks stood like weary sentinels, their facades scarred and faded by decades of harsh northern winters and neglect. Viktor Fyodorov approached one such relic—an imposing high-rise hastily thrown together during the Communist frenzy of the 1950s. The building groaned beneath the oppressive weight of years, its concrete shell mottled with cracked plaster and grimy streaks of pollution, windows fractured or clouded by dust and grime. The chipped metal handle of the entrance door was icy cold in his palm as he grasped it, a faint shiver tracing up his arm. When he pushed, the door protested with a screeching clang, the shrill cry of rusted hinges echoing down the dim, shadowed corridor beyond.

Inside, Viktor was immediately struck by the sour stench of rotting garbage wafting relentlessly from the refuse chute, a fetid wall that assaulted his senses and curled in the back of his throat. Each step up the narrow, grimy staircase churned the rancid odor anew, mingled with the faint, incessant hum of flies buzzing somewhere just beyond sight, the air thick and stagnant, barely stirred by a lazy draft sneaking through cracked windowpanes.

He reached the fifth floor, fingers trembling slightly as he produced the key worn smooth from years of use. Unlocking the door to the cramped apartment he shared with his brother's chaotic family, he was met by a stale, suffocating air that seemed as heavy as the burdens they all carried. Inside, the dim light revealed a world suspended between decay and desperation. His brother sprawled across the battered couch, motionless except for a faint wheeze in rhythm with the rising and falling of his chest. A half-empty bottle of vodka balanced precariously on his chest, glinting dully in the weak afternoon sun filtering through tattered curtains. The brother's eyes barely opened, offering only a half-hearted grunt in greeting as Viktor crossed the threshold, making no effort to lift his heavy head.

The kitchen—no refuge from the gloom—offered its own tableau of hardship. Natasja, his brother's wife, stood hunched before the ancient stove, her skeletal frame swaying slightly as she stirred a chipped and dented pot with slow, weary movements. A sharp tang of cheap alcohol clung to her like a mournful shadow, permeating the cramped room. She didn't glance up when Viktor entered, her eyes fixed on some distant point beyond the peeling wallpaper.

"Anything worth eating in there?" Viktor asked, his voice heavy with tired hope as he dropped onto one of the battered kitchen chairs. The wood creaked ominously beneath his weight, a small reminder of the apartment's crumbling infrastructure. Fatigue pressed down on him—both physical and emotional—as the familiar sights and smells pressed in like an unshakable fog.

Inside, he wrestled with the bitter ache of helplessness. Surrounded by stagnation and ruin, the struggle to hold together even the barest semblance of normal life weighed heavily on his shoulders. The decay whispered of dreams deferred and futures stolen—visions of a better life drowned by poverty, addiction, and resignation. Yet beneath the weariness flickered a stubborn ember of determination, a refusal to be wholly broken by the relentless grind of their existence.

Natasja merely grunted, a low, guttural sound lost somewhere in her throat, her response utterly unintelligible. The rhythmic, metallic clink-clink-clink of her spoon against the chipped pot was the only sound in the cramped, stifling room, a monotonous counterpoint to the quiet despair. Viktor rolled his eyes, a familiar gesture of resignation, and grabbed the tattered, dog-eared newspaper lying on the table. Its pages rustled softly as he skimmed the headlines, trying to decipher the stale news of a world far removed from their own. The faint, persistent smell of overcooked cabbage, heavy and cloying, clung to the air like a shroud, mingling with the ever-present undertones of stale alcohol and unwashed linen.

"At least tell me it's edible," he ventured, lowering the paper just enough to glance at her. Natasja continued her stirring, her back a rigid, unyielding line, not bothering to acknowledge him with even a flicker of her eyes. The silence that followed was not just quiet; it was a vast, stifling emptiness, filled only by the echoes of unspoken grievances and dreams long dead.

In that suffocating silence, Viktor's gaze drifted to the window, its pane streaked with grime and perpetually fogged, obscuring the world beyond. Through the blurred glass, the evening sky glowed a pale, ethereal pink, a fleeting moment of beauty cruelly marred by the stark, brutal outlines of identical, crumbling high-rises in the distance. They stood like skeletal fingers pointing accusingly at the heavens, monuments to a failed utopian vision. His eyes settled on the particularly gray, squat block directly across from their own—a constant, visual reminder of his fate. He thought of the fertilizer factory, a monstrous complex that loomed on the city's edge, spewing out not just chemicals but a soul-sucking monotony. It was a place that had consumed the lives of men like his father before him, grinding them down into dust, just as it was slowly, inexorably, consuming him.

"Another glorious day tomorrow," he muttered, the sarcasm thick and bitter, almost a physical presence in the air as he noted the deceptively clear sky. The irony burned. The clear sky doesn't mean anything. He will be locked in the factory, and must endure more of the same endless, grinding.

From the darkened cavern of the living room, his brother's slurred, distant voice cut through the quiet. "Still the factory drone, eh, Viktor? Same grind, different day." The words were heavy with the dull resignation of the perpetually drunk, yet carried a subtle, mocking edge.

"Factory doesn't clock out early for drunks," Viktor shot back, his voice surprisingly sharp, cutting through the stagnant air like a razor. He didn't look up from the crumpled newspaper, refusing to grant his brother the satisfaction of an acknowledged gaze. The words were automatic, born of years of resentment and the desperate need to assert some small measure of control.

His brother grumbled something incoherent, a shapeless sound of complaint, and then fell silent again, sinking back into his alcoholic stupor. Viktor shook his head slowly, a deep, weary sigh escaping him. He flipped the newspaper page with a snap, more forcefully than necessary, the small, sharp sound a futile attempt to shatter the suffocating silence and the heavy weight of his own bitter despair. He knew, with a certainty that gnawed at his gut, that he was capable of more than this. This life, this apartment, this pervasive stench of decay – it was a cage, and every day the bars felt tighter.

Natasja finally broke the oppressive silence, her voice flat and devoid of warmth. "Dinner's ready," she announced quietly, placing a steaming bowl of pale, grayish soup in front of Viktor. Her hands trembled ever so slightly, betraying a fatigue deeper than mere physical exhaustion. Without waiting for any reply, she turned back to the stove, her movements mechanical, as if driven by routine rather than any spark of hope or care.

Viktor stared down at the bowl, the thin, watery broth staring back at him like a bleak metaphor for his own existence— colorless, diluted, and devoid of nourishment. He picked up the spoon and poked listlessly at the surface, watching the faint curls of steam drift upward and dissolve into the stale air. His appetite had long since vanished, replaced by a gnawing emptiness that food could no longer fill.

Through the grimy window pane, his gaze drifted again to the distant horizon, where rows of decaying apartment blocks stretched out like concrete tombstones beneath a leaden sky. Beyond them, the looming silhouette of the fertilizer factory cast a dark shadow over the city. The plant had recently been acquired by a wealthy Moscow oligarch, one of the notorious "new elites" whose fortunes were built on shifting allegiances and ruthless ambition. Viktor couldn't begin to fathom what this change would mean for him or for any of the men trapped in the factory's endless grind. There was only one certainty—a bitter one—that it wouldn't make life any better, wouldn't ease the heavy yoke that bore down on those like him.

The thought settled heavily in his chest as he set the spoon down and pushed the bowl carefully aside, folding the crumpled newspaper with an absent-minded carelessness. In the corner, a battered radio emitted a low buzz, its monotonous voice droning on about politics and promises—words soaked in apathy and deceit, all irrelevant to the survival pressing at the edges of his world. Viktor's mind refused to engage; he could not summon the energy to care for empty speeches.

Tomorrow would come, bringing with it the same harsh routine. The same bitter monotony. The factory's whistle would sound again, and he would return to the soul-sucking workday that devoured his spirit bit by bit.

And so it would repeat.

As the next day waned, Viktor nodded curtly to his coworkers, the customary but hollow gesture of shared fatigue. "Goodbye!" he called out, the flatness in his voice belying the heaviness in his chest. The heavy steel door behind him slammed shut with a metallic clang that echoed forlornly across the factory yard—a somber farewell to another day swallowed by toil. Outside, his bike waited silently in the rack, its frame dulled beneath a thin veil of dust—an unwelcome residue from the factory's relentless haze. Unlocking it, he swung his leg over and started the familiar journey through Novgorod's bustling, chaotic streets.

The evening sun cast a warm amber glow that touched his soot-smudged face, offering a fleeting embrace of comfort against the grime that clung to his skin like a second skin. Behind him loomed the sprawling skeleton of the fertilizer factory—an industrial beast of weathered steel and crumbling concrete. Its twisted towers of pipes clawed skyward, their rust-streaked surfaces betraying decades of neglect. A faint haze of chemical vapor hovered in the air, omnipresent and invasive, sticking to his clothes and skin as a constant reminder of the suffocating hours spent within its unforgiving walls. The mechanical heartbeat of the factory—rhythmic thuds and grinding gears—pulsed in his memory, fused with the acrid tang of ammonia that had long since become a ghostly presence in his daily existence. Groups of workers, gaunt and weary, shuffled out in hushed clusters; their sunken faces and muted voices spoke of spirits drained beyond repair, casualties to a ceaseless grind far heavier than muscle and bone.

Ahead, on the cracked sidewalk, a mother clutched tightly to the hand of a little girl whose golden curls caught the last rays of sunlight, bouncing with innocent joy. The child's bright, carefree laughter floated above the muted hum of traffic—a piercing note of vitality amid the urban decay. Suddenly, without warning, the girl let go of her mother's grasp and bolted into the street—directly into Viktor's path.

"Damn it!" Viktor yelled, heart hammering as he yanked hard on the brakes. The tires screeched in protest, sending the bike wobbling dangerously on the uneven pavement before it ground to a halt mere inches from the child's small, trembling feet.

The mother rushed forward, face pallid with panic, words stumbling out in frantic apologies. "I'm so sorry! Are you— are you okay?" She clutched the girl's arm, whose wide eyes brimmed with fresh tears, trembling with shock. Viktor sucked in a ragged breath, adrenaline still thrumming fiercely through his veins, the sharp spike of fear slowly fading into a numb realization.

In that suspended moment, amidst the clatter of the city's evening rush, Viktor's mind wrestled with a storm of emotions—the relief of narrowly avoiding disaster, the overwhelming weight of responsibility, and a gnawing bitterness toward a life where danger lurked in every routine moment. The incident was a stark reminder that outside the factory's walls, peril wore many faces—not only the choking ammonia or grinding machinery, but fragile lives entwined with his own fragile existence on these unforgiving streets.

"It's fine," Viktor managed, forcing a tight, strained smile despite the adrenaline still hammering through his veins. The flush of near-disaster clung stubbornly to his skin, but he masked it well, unwilling to show weakness to the panicked mother or the innocent child who had unwittingly sprinted into danger.

A few blocks away, Viktor parked his bike outside a small, weathered kiosk tucked among the gray concrete buildings. The cracked door jingled a tired welcome as he stepped inside, the cramped interior saturated with the smell of newsprint and stale tobacco smoke. Shelves creaked beneath the weight of cluttered racks filled with magazines, newspapers, and battered paperback novels—a chaotic mosaic of fleeting interests and forgotten stories.

His eyes drifted across glossy covers, the gaudy colors and bold headlines clashing against the muted light. A magazine dedicated to foreign sports cars caught his attention, its pages alive with gleaming automobiles, their sleek lines and polished curves a stark contrast to the world he navigated daily. Viktor flipped through the pages, momentarily captivated by a distant dream of speed and escape, of a life far removed from factory grime and cramped apartments.

He fished a handful of rubles from his worn wallet, fingers rough and calloused, ready to pay. But then something else snagged his attention—a gossip magazine, its cover dominated by the stern, unyielding face of an older man. Bold headlines framed the image, promising scandal and power plays beneath the glossy surface. Viktor's brow furrowed as recognition clicked into place. So that's the new owner, he thought, studying the cold, calculating eyes of Boris Jumashyev, the oligarch who had recently purchased the factory where Viktor toiled.

Such magazines were usually beneath him—sensationalist drivel not worth the ink—but a flicker of curiosity, mingled with cautious unease, tugged at him. With a faint sigh, he nodded to the shopkeeper. "I'll take this one too," he said, dropping it onto the counter next to the sports car magazine, a small concession to the intrigue swirling unseen beneath his quiet exterior.

Back at the apartment, the familiar staleness welcomed him like an old, begrudging acquaintance. The air inside was heavy and unmoving, thick with the scent of unwashed bodies and lingering smoke. The dim, worn interior seemed to sag under the weight of years and hardship. His brother lay sprawled on the frayed couch, snoring softly despite the bottle balanced precariously on the edge of the battered coffee table—a fragile equilibrium between oblivion and neglect.

From the kitchen, faint clatters of pans and dishes echoed, the steady rhythm pointing to Natasja's relentless efforts to maintain some semblance of normalcy. Her presence, muted and weary, was a quiet undercurrent running beneath the apartment's chaos, offering a fragile tether to routine in lives teetering on the edge.

As Viktor sank into a chair, lifting the papers and magazines, the contrast between his day's trivial indulgences and the grim reality around him pressed heavily on his mind. Each page a reminder of worlds beyond reach—and the tightening grip of survival that shaped every waking moment he endured.

"Dinner," Viktor muttered as a passing greeting, his voice low and subdued as he moved past his sister-in-law, Natasja. She was hunched over the stove, her silhouette etched against the dim kitchen light. The faint aroma of something simmering rose from the pot, mingling with the lingering scent of damp wood and stale air that clung stubbornly to the aging apartment. The kitchen felt heavy and worn, every surface marked by years of use and neglect, a quiet testament to their shared, hard-fought survival.

[35]

"I bought a magazine," Viktor added, settling into a creaky kitchen chair that groaned beneath him. His voice carried a little more strength this time, but he doubted he'd break through Natasja's silence. She cast a brief, unreadable glance over her shoulder, the faintest flicker of something—weariness, resignation, perhaps—passing across her face before she turned back to her task, stirring the pot with mechanical precision.

Viktor opened the car magazine first, seeking a moment's escape. The glossy photos of gleaming Ferraris, Lamborghinis, and sleek Mercedes filled the pages with an unreachable glamour. For a fleeting instant, he imagined the cool leather of a steering wheel beneath his fingers, the hum of a powerful engine responding to his touch, the open road stretching ahead like a promise. But the fantasy dissolved almost as quickly as it came, replaced by the sharp pang of his reality—those cars were distant symbols, desires reserved for a world to which he did not belong. A wistful sigh escaped him, louder than intended, and caused Natasja to pause and glance his way once more. He met her gaze only briefly before turning the page, burying his longing deeper.

The gossip magazine sat unopened until he finished with the car glossy, its vivid colors now more stark, almost mocking. When he finally turned to it, he was drawn again to the profile of Boris Jumashyev—the new owner of the fertilizer factory that had dominated Viktor's life for years. The glossy image showed Boris surrounded by signs of wealth and power Viktor barely understood: sleek limousines, opulent offices, the kind of excess that felt alien and foreboding. Beside Boris stood his daughter—a young woman in her mid-twenties—whose poised, confident demeanor marked her as a product of a world far removed from Viktor's cramped apartment and daily grind. The sharp edges of their lives seemed to reflect a chasm growing ever wider between two starkly different realities.

In that cramped kitchen, with its peeling paint and flickering bulb, Viktor felt the weight of the divide pressing down harder than ever—a gulf measured not only in wealth, but in opportunity, hope, and escape. The magazines were more than mere distractions; they were windows into a life tantalizingly close, yet painfully out of reach. And with every turn of their glossy pages, the quiet anguish of his own existence deepened.

Viktor squinted at the photograph—Jelena Jumashyeva. She wasn't what he expected of a woman born into privilege; not a dazzling beauty, but something subtler held his gaze. Her face carried a calm poise and quiet confidence, the kind of effortless grace that seemed natural to those who navigate a world built on wealth and influence. The soft lines of her jaw and the steady set of her eyes suggested a person shaped by expectation and refinement, yet beneath that veneer lingered an inscrutable depth—an allure that stirred something guarded yet restless in Viktor's chest.

The article spread out before him detailed snippets of her life: a political science student in Moscow, a devoted tennis player, and her summer plans to visit her father. These fragments painted a picture of a life so removed from his own hardships—one filled with ambition and delicate freedoms he barely dared imagine. The world she inhabited was defined by privileges that shaped opportunities at every turn, while his days were consumed by relentless labor and survival.

Viktor's finger hovered over her image, fingertips tracing the contours of her face in a tentative, almost reverent gesture, as if trying to pull something tangible from the printed page—a connection, a meaning beyond mere curiosity. Her expression, poised yet softly reserved, held a quiet allure he couldn't articulate, but one that resonated deep within him, stirring a complicated mix of admiration, longing, and the aching gulf between their disparate realities.

In the dim light of his cramped apartment, surrounded by the smells of overcooked food and stale air, the glossy magazine felt like a fragile portal to a world both tantalizingly close and heartbreakingly distant. As Viktor wrestled with the silent ache of his own restricted existence, Jelena's image became more than a picture—it became a symbol of everything he yearned for and everything barred from reach.

Chapter 4

Viktor lifted his gaze from the rumbling machines, letting it wander across the worn, familiar walls of the factory where he'd labored since leaving school. The day was nearly over, and a crushing exhaustion weighed on him like a shackle, dragging him down step by weary step. I've logged so many overtime hours lately—no one will notice if I slip out a few minutes early today, he reasoned, his thoughts already drifting toward the exit and the tantalizing promise of freedom beyond the factory doors.

But just as his hand reached for the cold, metal handle, a furious voice shattered the silence. Sergej Nikolajevitsj stormed over, his eyes blazing with contempt. "Move your lazy ass, you good-for-nothing slacker! This isn't some damn rest home!" he growled, jabbing a grimy finger inches from Viktor's face, his lips curling into a smug, disdainful sneer.

A surge of heat rushed through Viktor's veins; a fierce wave of anger swelled inside him, clenching his fists tightly. He was fed up with Sergej's ceaseless contempt. Sergej, barely forty, yet worn and weathered—his face lined with bitterness, clothes hanging loose on his wiry frame—had grown only harsher since his recent promotion to foreman. He seemed to take a twisted delight in picking apart every worker beneath him. That daily grind of humiliation gnawed relentlessly at Viktor's patience.

"Go to hell!" Viktor spat back, his voice taut with fury, locking eyes with Sergej's pompous, sneering face.

Around them, other workers gathered, some shaking their heads in silent warning. Viktor knew what they thought— that swallowing one's pride was safer than risking the loss of a job. But he was tired. So very tired of swallowing his pride.

Sergej's face flushed a deep, violent red, mouth parting to unleash another torrent of venom. But before he could speak, sharp, angry voices boomed from outside the factory—harsh and hostile.

Viktor's gut twisted in dread as men exchanged worried glances, faces drawn tight with fear and confusion. Without warning, some grabbed shovels, pipes, and metal rods and surged toward the exit, propelled by a wild urgency.

For a moment, Viktor froze, dread rooting him in place. Then his burning anger propelled him forward. Grabbing a heavy wrench, his pulse thundered in his chest—a sickening blend of fear and fury.

Outside, the air was thick and oppressive, hot with sweat and tension. The sight before Viktor's eyes made his blood run cold. Beyond the gates stood a mob—forty, maybe fifty men—armed with rifles, clubs, and bats. Their eyes glinted with menace as they hurled insults and clawed at the gate, yanking at the thick chains that bound it shut. A few were already scrambling over the fence, their combined weight twisting and snapping the old metal with a wrenching clang. The mob surged forward like a violent tide, shots rang out, and fists and weapons collided in a brutal cacophony. The workers staggered back, retreating step by step into the factory, terror sharp and raw as they braced against the relentless assault.

Viktor found himself on the edge of the chaos, wild and helpless terror rising in his chest. His mind raced. What do they want? Are they here to seize the factory by force? The thought sent icy chills down his spine as he envisioned the one place they relied on for their livelihoods falling into criminal hands. Rumors had circulated for years about factories taken violently—workers cast out in brutal coups. Viktor knew that once criminals took control, reclaiming what was lost was almost impossible. Courts, slow and often corrupt, moved only as fast as the bribes allowed. He'd seen how the system favored those with power and money. The men bursting through the gates wouldn't stop until they had everything.

He gritted his teeth, fingers tightening on the wrench as his thoughts turned to recent changes at the factory. A powerful oligarch from Moscow had seized control, profits surged, and the factory had become an even bigger target. Yet Viktor never imagined anyone would dare to challenge Moscow's influence so brazenly.

Suddenly, sharp, searing pain exploded in his ribs—a blunt force striking him and sending him sprawling backward. He hit the ground hard, breath knocked out of him. Blinking through shock, he looked up to see one of the intruders looming above, a mocking sneer twisting his face, rifle raised in one hand. Viktor's breath caught, mixing terror and a fierce, burning fury. He wouldn't go down like this—he wouldn't be reduced to nothing. In a single, desperate motion, he sprang to his feet and drove a fierce kick into his attacker's groin.

The man's scream tore through the thick air as he doubled over, clutching himself in agony. Viktor didn't hesitate for a moment. Clenching the wrench with both hands, he summoned every ounce of strength left in his battered body, refusing to surrender. Panic and adrenaline blurred his senses as he swung the wrench with brutal force. His heart hammered wildly in his chest the instant the wrench slammed into the man's body.

Without missing a beat, he kicked the rifle away, his breath ragged and uneven. His hands trembled, but he raised the wrench again, swinging it into soft flesh with a sickening thud.

A ragged, strangled sigh escaped the man's lips as he crumpled to the ground, motionless.

Viktor froze, his entire body rigid with shock and fear, staring down at the lifeless figure. His pulse thundered in his ears as he slowly backed away, his eyes darting nervously. He snagged the rifle from the ground, gripping it with a white-knuckled intensity. His mind raced—What if they come for me next?

But no one seemed to notice him. Shaken, he stumbled toward the factory doorway.

Just as he reached the threshold, a piercing wail rent the air— the sirens blared to life, slicing through the chaos. The sound was deafening, jagged and relentless. Viktor clapped his hands tightly over his ears, trembling as the noise seemed to reverberate deep through his bones.

Inside the entrance, a truck sat waiting, its dull metal gleaming dully under the harsh lights. Viktor's heart hammered wildly as he darted toward it. The driver's door of the Volvo creaked open, and he peered inside. The keys gleamed in the ignition, still untouched.

Without a second thought, he threw himself into the driver's seat, hands shaking violently as he scrambled to start the engine.

He'd never driven a vehicle this massive before, but somehow, through sheer force of will, he managed to rev the engine without stalling. His breath came in ragged gasps as the truck roared to life—a growl of power beneath his anxious hands. What now? What was he supposed to do?

His jaw clenched tight as he slammed his foot down on the accelerator. The truck surged forward with the weight and momentum of a living beast, charging out of the building and toward the hostile crowd.

Gunfire erupted in a harsh staccato as the attackers opened fire on the truck.

Viktor ducked low between the seat and the steering wheel, his heart hammering as bullets tore into the metal around him. Glass shattered explosively like a hailstorm, but all he could see was swirling chaos. With a desperate, frantic yank, he twisted the wheel hard, sending the truck skidding sideways into the mob.

Dust exploded around him, billowing like a living, choking wall. The screams of pain sliced through the air—jagged, shrill cries—as men were struck down. Some were flung onto the hood, their bodies tossed like ragdolls into the air. Others were crushed beneath the relentless weight of the tires.

Viktor's stomach churned violently; his hands locked on the wheel, knuckles white as bone, trembling in the grip of pure terror. Time stretched and slowed, seconds bleeding into endless moments before the truck finally screeched to a halt.

He sat frozen, shaking, breath ragged and uneven. His mind was a chaotic blur. Had he hit his own people? Was this his fault?

His hands trembled as they reached down, clutching the rifle on the floor beside him. He peered cautiously over the door, eyes wide and searching.

The world outside had dissolved into utter chaos. Men were still locked in violent struggle; lifeless bodies lay scattered across the ground—some groaning weakly, others screaming in pain.

Then, like a thunderclap, a roar of police sirens shattered the frenzied noise. A squad of police cars screeched to an abrupt halt, blocking the factory entrance. Dark-clad officers armed with automatic weapons spilled out, moving swiftly and purposefully toward the building.

Relief flooded Viktor's chest so fiercely he could have wept. It was the anti-terror unit—they had come to help.

But the gunfire didn't cease.

Viktor's blood ran cold as a gangster leapt onto the truck's running board, leaning in, eyes wild and filled with hatred.

Instinct surged forward unbidden. Viktor squeezed the trigger. A burst of gunfire tore through the man's face with a chilling finality. The gangster's body slumped forward, half inside the cab. Blood poured from the wound in his neck, soaking Viktor's shirt, the warmth chilling him to the bone as it dripped onto his skin.

"Oh, dear Virgin Mary…" Viktor muttered, his throat tight and dry. Bile rose in his throat, but he forced himself not to look away. Sweat poured down his face, palms slick with moisture as he gripped the rifle tighter.

Seconds later, the door was yanked open from outside. The dead gangster's body was dumped onto the ground like a sack of heavy potatoes. A man clad in black stared into the cab, locking eyes with Viktor.

"Out!" the officer barked sharply, weapon raised, signaling Viktor to get out immediately.

Viktor nodded, legs trembling like jelly as he scrambled to escape the truck. Before he could even touch the ground, a rough hand seized the back of his shirt, yanking him violently and throwing him harshly onto the gravel. He slammed down chin-first, a strangled scream tearing from his throat as a sharp, searing pain shot through his body. The coarse gravel scraped and gouged his skin, forcing his arms wide and legs splayed in a helpless, sprawling heap. He lay frozen, barely breathing, the cold, unforgiving steel of a rifle barrel pressing hard against the back of his head.

"Get up!"

The voice was a low, menacing hiss, dripping with iron authority. The command barely penetrated Viktor's fog of terror; his senses felt numb, his mind spinning in a haze. Only when the man gripped him roughly by the collar, yanking him halfway to his feet, did the weight of the order finally settle in.

"You can get up." The words were short, firm, and unwavering before the man released him, melting back into the swirling chaos around them.

Viktor stumbled forward, blinking against the haze of dust and shock, his eyes wide with horror at the devastation unfolding around him. Bodies—his coworkers—were strewn across the ground, some lifeless, others writhing in agony, their agonized moans drifting through choking dust and muffled cries. For a heartbeat, Viktor stood rooted to the spot, legs suddenly unable to move, the crushing weight of fear pinning him down. His heart pounded fiercely in his chest as the raw, overwhelming reality crashed over him.

But with a choking swallow, he forced back rising panic, steadying his trembling hands. Drawing a deep, ragged breath, he fought through the wave of nausea and braced himself, staggering forward with grim determination—ready to help however he could amid the brutal devastation.

Chapter 5

By the next day, the production of artificial fertilizer had resumed its relentless pace, the factory humming back to life as if the prior chaos had been nothing more than a distant nightmare. Viktor was briefly celebrated as a hero; newspapers lauded his courage, and even the notoriously grumpy foreman managed to mutter a rare, begrudging "thank you." But the applause, like the headlines, quickly faded, swallowed whole by the unyielding, monotonous rhythm of daily life. The week trudged on, each day melting indistinguishably into the next, echoing the ceaseless, mechanical drone of the factory's machines.

On Sunday, Viktor awoke suddenly, his sleep fractured by something fleeting yet unsettling—an elusive disturbance he couldn't quite place. His eyes flicked to the alarm clock perched on the nightstand. The red digits glowed faintly: eight o'clock. Too early. He frowned, disoriented, grasping at the thin thread of memory. Was it a sound? A bad dream? He couldn't recall, but the weight in his chest lingered, heavy and oppressive.

He lay still, staring blankly at the ceiling above him—dull, lifeless, and unchanging, a mirror of his unsettled thoughts. Outside, the rain that had battered the windows all through the night was finally easing. Through streaked glass, he glimpsed faint patches of clearing sky. Streaks of pale blue pierced the gray clouds, while the sun hovered uncertainly, shifting back and forth between retreat and brilliance.

Eventually, Viktor forced himself out of bed, movements slow and mechanical, as if some invisible force pressed down on his limbs. He shuffled into the cramped bathroom and splashed cold water onto his face. The icy chill made him shiver but failed to wash away the heaviness lodged deep inside.

On the shelf above the sink, his contact lenses lay untouched from the night before. He picked them up and slid them into his eyes with the automatic precision of habit. Leaning closer to the mirror, he studied his reflection with weary eyes. An oval face stared back at him, plain and unremarkable. His dark brown hair, cropped short and practical, offered no distraction. His teeth, uneven and faintly yellowed, bore the dull stains of too many cigarettes and endless cups of bitter coffee. His ice-gray eyes, with pupils so dark they seemed nearly black, held no spark, no flicker of life or energy. They stared back—their gaze empty and resigned.

"I'm twenty-six years old and in my prime," he muttered under his breath, forcing a faint, hollow smile that felt absurd in the suffocating silence. The smile dissolved as quickly as it had appeared.

He combed his hair back, smoothing it down with a slow, distracted motion, then turned toward the bathroom cabinet. Hanging neatly on the door was a freshly pressed shirt. He slipped it on deliberately, the crisp fabric offering a faint semblance of routine, a fragile anchor in the turmoil of his mind.

In the kitchen, the thermometer perched on the windowsill already registered twenty-five degrees, though the morning was still young. Sunlight poured in through the window, flooding the room with a harsh, unyielding brightness that felt almost mocking, as if the world outside moved on indifferent to his inner struggle.

"It's far too nice a day to stay inside," Viktor said, attempting to inject some cheer into his voice. The effort fell flat—the words hollow and empty even to himself.

His brother, slouched over the kitchen table, barely acknowledged him. He muttered something indistinct, poured himself a glass of vodka, and sank deeper into his chair. With one hand loosely gripping the glass, he stared blankly at the sunlit world beyond the window, his eyes glazed and distant.

Viktor shrugged, a small, defeated gesture. There was no point in saying more. He reached for two dry slices of bread and spread a thin layer of liver pâté over them. Standing by the counter, he ate in silence. The bread was stale and tasteless, providing little more than the barest sustenance.

"I'm heading out," he said, grabbing a light jacket from a hook. "Sure you don't want to come along?"

His brother didn't respond, and Viktor didn't wait for a reply. The man's world revolved entirely around his vodka glass, and no words could penetrate that orbit.

Outside, the heat hit Viktor like a physical wall. He untied his jacket and draped it loosely over his shoulders as he stepped into the empty street. Aimless, he wandered with no destination, letting his feet carry him wherever.

The streets grew quieter, cleaner as he drifted into the wealthier parts of the city. Here, grand villas stood behind tall, imposing fences and lush, meticulously trimmed evergreen hedges, their facades gleaming under the sharp sunlight. Through gaps in the greenery, Viktor caught fleeting glimpses of polished windows and manicured lawns—silent, unspoken reminders of a world he could see but never touch.

The further he walked, the more out of place he felt. His scuffed shoes and weary gait seemed like glaring intrusions here—unwelcome marks of a reality these streets preferred to erase. Turning onto a quiet cul-de-sac, Viktor found himself on a street that didn't flaunt its wealth but radiated it subtly in every detail—the neatness, the order, the quiet perfection.

At the end of the street, a park stretched out, its emerald lawns lush and meticulously maintained. A dark limousine rolled smoothly past him, its heavily tinted windows concealing the lives within. The car eased to a stop just ahead, and the rear door swung open.

A woman stepped out—young, about his age, dressed entirely in crisp white. In one hand, she held a tennis racket; in the other, a sports bag hung casually over her shoulder.

Viktor froze. His breath caught in his throat as recognition dawned. For a long moment, he stood rooted to the spot, watching her. She moved with quiet confidence, each step deliberate and poised as she made her way toward the park. The sharp lines of her outfit, her graceful demeanor—it was as if she carried the weight of a world Viktor would never belong to.

His eyes followed her along the pathway. He had recognized her immediately—it was Jelena Jumashyeva, the daughter of the new owner of the fertilizer factory. Without hesitation, Viktor began to trail her, keeping a careful distance, blending into the background, making sure not to be seen.

After just a few minutes, the tennis courts came into view. The facility looked brand new, its pristine courts already alive with activity. From two or three hundred meters away, Viktor could clearly hear the rhythmic thwack of rackets striking bright yellow tennis balls.

Jelena approached the court where a young woman dressed in white sat on a bench nearby. The woman scanned the area, her face lighting up as she spotted Jelena.

"Hey!" she called out cheerfully. "Finally, you're here!"

The two women embraced, laughter spilling between them as if no time had passed since their last meeting.

Viktor slowed his pace and stopped about twenty meters away. He stood silently, watching their easy banter and lively laughter—a stark contrast to his quiet, solitary observation. Eventually, they moved to opposite sides of the court, taking their positions to begin the match.

Nearby, a medium-sized oak tree offered a patch of shade. Viktor sank down at its base, leaning his back against the rough, textured trunk. The grass beneath him was still damp with morning dew, cool and comforting despite the heat. From here, he had a perfect vantage point to watch the tennis courts unfold before him.

The match began, the bright yellow tennis ball slicing through the air with mounting speed. Jelena's movements were fluid and assured, her focus razor-sharp. Viktor

[51]

couldn't tear his eyes away, admiring the faint sun-kissed glow of her arms and legs as she played. Her opponent matched her skill shot for shot, returning each ball with precision and grace.

Suddenly, Jelena mis-hit the ball, sending it hurtling awkwardly toward Viktor. Startled, he sprang to his feet, catching it deftly in mid-air. Without thinking, he tossed it back onto the court. Jelena turned toward him, her face lighting up with a radiant smile.

"Thanks," she said, her voice warm and genuine as she settled back into position at the service line.

Viktor watched intently as she tossed the ball high into the air, her racket sweeping upward in a graceful arc before striking it with surprising force. The ball zipped across the net like a bullet. He admired the effortless blend of power and elegance in her every move. Both women were undeniably striking, a perfect picture of athleticism and grace.

As the match wore on, Viktor grew bolder, edging closer to the court. He wove his fingers through the green mesh of the fence, eyes glued to the game. Jelena and her opponent switched sides, bringing Jelena to the half nearest him. Viktor's gaze stayed fixed on her, a mix of awe and nervous anticipation swelling in his chest. He silently wished she might approach him, even for a brief conversation, though the thought churned in him with equal parts excitement and dread.

Jelena stepped up to serve. Her movements were smooth, practiced—almost hypnotic. She launched the ball into the air with delicate ease, sending it hurtling toward her opponent in a perfect arc. The return came fast and sharp, skimming just over the net. Jelena dashed forward, feet a blur as she lunged for the ball. But then, disaster struck—her footing slipped unexpectedly. With a sharp cry, she tumbled to the ground, clutching her ankle.

Viktor's heart leapt into his throat. He let go of the fence and sprinted onto the court without hesitation.

"Are you hurt? Did you break something?" he asked urgently, crouching beside her, panic coloring his voice.

"No, I don't think so," Jelena replied through a wince, struggling to stand. Her friend hurried over, offering a steadying hand. Jelena leaned heavily on her but clearly grimaced with pain.

"Can you make it to the bench?" Viktor asked gently, extending a hand.

Jelena nodded and, with Viktor supporting one side and her friend the other, hobbled toward the bench. Carefully, Viktor removed her shoe, hands trembling as he examined her swollen ankle.

"This doesn't look good. You might have a fracture," he said, casting a worried glance at her friend, who was already speaking urgently into her phone.

"You need to come immediately," the friend said before ending the call.

Moments later, a uniformed chauffeur appeared, striding quickly toward them. Together, he and Jelena's friend helped her to her feet and guided her away.

"Wait," Viktor called out, jogging to catch up. He scribbled his phone number on a scrap of paper and pressed it into Jelena's hand. "Let me know how your ankle is, okay?" Jelena looked at him, a mixture of surprise and gratitude softening her features. She nodded before being led away.

Viktor stood frozen for a moment, clutching the court's railing as he watched her disappear.

For the rest of the day, his phone remained within arm's reach. Every vibration made his heart leap, but Jelena did not call.

By Monday morning, silence still hung heavy. "Of course not," he muttered bitterly to himself as he pedaled to work. "Why would someone like her ever reach out to someone like me?"

During lunch, the workers gathered as usual in the cafeteria. "We're expecting an important visitor today. The new owner has taken a break from his hectic life in Moscow and will be visiting the factory," the foreman announced. Most workers barely registered the news, their chatter continuing as before. Viktor, however, listened closely.

"Do you think we'll get to meet him?" he asked Igor, the man seated closest.

Igor shrugged lazily. "Who? The new owner?" he said, glancing disinterestedly at Viktor.

Viktor nodded.

"I doubt it," Igor replied slowly. "He worked here as a director once—must've been in the 1980s, until around '90 or '91. Even then, he didn't give a damn about talking to us workers."

An hour later, a group of five or six sharply dressed men prowled briskly across the factory floor, led by a man in his sixties who barely spared a glance around. Viktor, in the middle of his tasks, recognized them immediately. His curiosity flared, but as they vanished behind a door, he reluctantly turned back to his work.

Igor had been right, Viktor thought bitterly as the door clanged shut behind them. Workers like them didn't matter at all.

When the shift ended, Viktor packed his things and left the dusty, noisy factory behind. The sun still hung high overhead. He made his way to the bike rack shaded by large, leafy trees where his blue-green bicycle was chained securely. Armed guards, ever-present since the attack, stood silently near the gate, their watchful eyes never wavering.

Viktor had just swung his leg over the blue-green frame of his bike when the new owner and his entourage emerged from the factory building. The suited men moved with practiced urgency, climbing swiftly into two sleek Mercedes-Benz cars parked near the entrance.

As Viktor neared the factory gate, the roar of engines thundered behind him. The cars sped past, their polished mirrors skimming dangerously close to his handlebars.

Damn it, he thought bitterly, glaring at the fading taillights. They wouldn't have even stopped if they'd run me over.

At home, Viktor slammed the door shut behind him and trudged up the narrow staircase. During dinner, he sat silently, his mind adrift in faraway thoughts. Once the meal ended, he retreated to his room without a word and collapsed onto the bed. The apartment echoed with the shrill voices of his younger siblings—the teenagers fighting noisily over a video game, their laughter and shouts piercing through the thin walls.

He turned away from the noise, pressing his face into the pillow, trying to block it all out. As usual, Jelena Jumashyeva's face flooded his mind—her soft brown eyes, the warm glow of her slightly sun-kissed skin, the faintest trace of sweat and deodorant clinging to her.

He could still feel the delicate weight of her slender frame as she leaned on him, and hear the soft pain underlying her voice. The brief, reluctant nod she gave when she accepted his note.

A groan escaped his lips as he buried his face deeper into the pillow. Why couldn't he stop thinking about her? She's never going to call, he thought bitterly. Someone like her would never care about someone like me.

The room felt suffocating, the cluttered, faded patterns on the worn wallpaper mocking him silently as his mind spiraled again into the same hopeless realization that gripped him every day. He hated the crushing oppression of poverty, the relentless monotony of a life with no escape.

His parents had lived in the same bleak, hopeless cycle until the day they died. His father had been ground down endlessly by the unforgiving demands of the fertilizer factory in Novgorod. Now Viktor was trapped on that same path, his life slipping ever closer to an echo of his father's despair.

Every evening, his father drowned his sorrows in vodka, pouring glass after glass as if to quench an unrelenting, smoldering fire inside. Viktor couldn't blame him. As he stared at the chaotic swirls of peeling wallpaper, he thought maybe vodka was the only way his father had managed to endure such a wretched existence. But the relief came at a devastating cost. His father had succumbed to cirrhosis before even reaching fifty, leaving Viktor and his siblings orphaned.

Their mother had been gone for years already, but her memory clung to Viktor like a ghost—vivid, unyielding, haunting.

One afternoon, without warning or explanation, the police had stormed their home and taken her away. Viktor was only seven then, but the searing image was etched deep in his mind: his mother clinging desperately to his father while he, a small, frightened boy, wrapped his tiny arms tightly around her legs, refusing to let go.

What kind of world—what kind of merciless society—rips a mother away from her children? Her only crime had been selling a few handmade dresses she had sewn in secret, in stolen moments. The state showed no leniency, no mercy. Found guilty of operating an unregistered private business, she was sentenced to two years in prison—two years for selling dresses.

"Mama…" he whispered, voice barely audible, trembling as a crushing wave of sorrow swept through him. The memory of her kindness, her warmth, remained sharp. She was a free spirit, fiercely loving her family but unable to endure the suffocating confinement.

Just weeks after her deportation, the cruel news had come— a death knell that shattered what remained of their fragile family. She had hanged herself in her cell.

Chapter 6

The next day, Viktor skipped work for the first time in his life. The decision weighed heavily on him, an uneasy knot twisting relentlessly in his stomach. Vladimir Tersakov, an old schoolmate, had called late the previous night with a proposition. At first, Viktor refused outright—the idea struck him as reckless, even foolish. But as the night stretched on, the thought gnawed at him, growing less absurd with every passing hour. By morning, curiosity had won out.

He cycled past the restaurant Vladimir had mentioned. Viktor didn't recognize the place, but it was clearly popular. In the brief moments it took him to ride by, he caught sight of several people coming and going, their laughter and lively chatter drifting toward him—a sharp, almost painful contrast to the oppressive silence that clung to his own existence.

At the corner, Viktor dismounted and approached a small kiosk, buying an ice cream cone. Wandering back, he settled onto a bench in the square across from the restaurant, the cone slowly melting in his hands. The restaurant occupied the entire ground floor of a three-story, gray-white stone building. The upper floors were residential; several windows stood open, offering glimpses of worn furniture inside. Viktor squinted, attempting to count how many cramped apartments might fill the old block, but lost interest halfway through, distracted by the muted hum of life around him.

A sharp gust stirred the air, kicking up dust and sending it swirling into his face. A stray newspaper skidded across the pavement, looping around his foot. Irritated, Viktor shook it off with a swift kick. The biting dust scratched at his throat and tickled his nose, forcing a grimace.

A scrappy, scrawny dog trotted over and flopped down obediently in front of him, tail wagging hesitantly, its brown eyes fixed on every bite Viktor took. With a sigh, Viktor broke off a small piece of the cone and tossed it toward the eager mutt. "Surviving the only way you know how, huh?" he muttered under his breath. The dog devoured the piece in seconds, tail thumping in eager anticipation of more.

Viktor rose, crumpled the ice cream wrapper, and tossed it into a nearby trash can. The dog gave him one last hopeful glance before trotting off down the street.

He locked his bicycle to a rusted, worn lamppost just outside the restaurant and wandered down the sidewalk. The street narrowed, leading to a quieter alley at the far end of the block. Turning the corner, he found himself behind the restaurant. A weathered, rotting wooden fence separated the alley from a grimy back courtyard.

Through a narrow crack between the planks, Viktor spotted several garbage bins lined up against the building's peeling, battered wall. A battered door, stained brown and leaning crookedly against its frame, hinted at years of neglect—the varnish long faded and flaking. Above it, sagging windows loomed like tired eyes, their cracked panes refracting the weak sunlight with a dull, fractured glow.

He studied the dilapidated facade, mind racing with uneasy thoughts. Breaking in wouldn't be difficult. With trembling fingers, he pulled out his phone and dialed. "Hey," he said when Vladimir answered. "It's Viktor. If you still need me, I'm in."

Two days later, in the bitter cold of the night, Viktor stood shivering beside Vladimir at the same decaying fence. The air was bone-chilling, a biting wind slashing sharply through the narrow alley, setting a loose gate clanging intermittently somewhere deeper in the shadows.

Above them, the sky was an ominous slate gray, thick with heavy storm clouds that seemed to press down on the quiet street. Their breaths rose in ghostly plumes, quickly dissipating in the icy air.

Viktor shoved his numbing hands deep into his pockets, but the cold did little to calm the dread spreading through his chest. What in God's name was he doing here? He tried to steady his trembling nerves, but the mounting weight of Vladimir's scheme pressed heavily upon him. The alley was deathly still, save for the rhythmic banging of the gate somewhere nearby.

Somewhere in the distance, a dog barked sharply—a short, piercing sound that made Viktor flinch. He glanced sideways at Vladimir, who seemed impervious to the cold or the tension that thickened the air. If Vladimir noticed Viktor's unease, he gave no sign. As the minutes dragged on, Viktor's certainty deepened: he had made a terrible mistake.

He studied the worn, crumbling façade once again. Despite the chill, several windows on the second and third floors stood slightly ajar. Likely, people were still asleep behind those walls. He would have to move with utmost silence, each step carefully calculated to avoid waking them. The thought made his palms inexplicably damp with sweat despite the icy air around him. His breath fogged as he crossed the rickety fence, the soles of his shoes crunching softly on scattered gravel.

Vladimir was already ahead, crouched near the entrance like a shadow melting into the darkness. In his hand, he held a set of lockpicks, the slender tools gleaming faintly under the weak glow of a streetlamp. With smooth, precise movements, he unlatched the door and motioned sharply for Viktor to follow.

Inside, the narrow hallway was dimly lit by a single bare bulb that buzzed faintly overhead. The air was thick with the smell of mildew and something metallic beneath it. Vladimir moved forward with deliberate steps, their shadows stretching long and distorted along the grimy walls. They slipped silently through a swinging door into the pitch-black kitchen.

Viktor hesitated for a moment before clicking on his flashlight. Its narrow beam cut through the darkness, illuminating a heavy wooden block on the counter, bristling with knives. Vladimir approached it, his figure a dark silhouette. He pulled two blades free, turning them carefully to examine the edges. Seeing his dark-clad friend wield cold steel sent a chill crawling down Viktor's spine.

"Here. Take this," Vladimir whispered, voice low but firm.

Viktor hesitated as the knife was pressed into his hand. It felt heavier than it should, the cold steel gleaming like an accusing blade. His body stiffened.

"Take it!" Vladimir hissed sharply, shoving the knife forward.

Reluctantly, Viktor gritted his teeth against the urge to drop it and accepted the blade. The metal was cold and alien in his grip, its weight anchoring his hand with an unsettling heaviness. He followed Vladimir out of the kitchen, the weight of the knife a constant pull.

They ascended the creaking staircase, footsteps quiet but steady. Vladimir moved with the grace of a predator, clearly familiar with the labyrinthine building. Without hesitation, he led them directly to the third floor.

They stopped outside a door. Vladimir ran his fingers smoothly over the worn handle before working the lock with practiced efficiency. The door creaked open, releasing a wave of stale, heavy air. The scent of fried fish and onions lingered thickly, clinging to the walls in an oppressive fog.

Viktor swallowed hard as his flashlight swept the cramped, dim space—a small room, a tiny kitchen, and a bathroom cramped into the limited quarters. Against the far wall, beneath a curtainless window, a young man lay sprawled across a worn sofa, his chest rising and falling in a steady but shallow rhythm.

Vladimir pulled a length of rough rope from his pocket and moved silently toward the sleeping figure. Viktor's flashlight beam wavered with his unsteady hand as he watched. Vladimir was cold and methodical, a predator cloaked in shadow.

As the young man stirred, Vladimir swiftly slipped the rope around his neck and tightened his grip. The man's eyes snapped open wide; panic surged as his hands clawed frantically at the constricting rope. A guttural choke tore from his throat as his body twisted fiercely, fighting with desperate strength.

In a wild, sudden movement, he kicked sharply, his heel connecting with Vladimir's face with a sickening crack. Vladimir stumbled, momentarily stunned, his grip loosening under the unexpected blow. Another powerful kick sent Vladimir reeling backward. Seizing the moment, the young man lunged forward, wrenching the rope free with frantic, shaking hands.

Viktor froze, his feet suddenly rooted to the cold, grimy floor. The young man lunged at Vladimir with desperate fury, slamming his head against the hard surface with a brutal, echoing thud that reverberated sharply in Viktor's ears. The sound jolted him into motion. Heart pounding wildly, he surged forward, the knife trembling violently in his unsteady hand.

"Stop!" Viktor shouted, panic fracturing his voice. The cold blade pressed against the young man's throat, shaking uncontrollably, carried by the intensity of Viktor's fear.

But the young man fought back fiercely. His foot swept out in a sharp, sudden kick, striking Viktor hard in the stomach. The impact sent Viktor stumbling backward, the knife grazing the man's neck in the chaos. Time seemed to slow as dark, relentless blood gushed from the wound—warm and unforgiving—pooling rapidly on the floor in growing, ominous circles.

The young man's hands flew to his wounded throat, eyes wide with mounting terror and shock. He staggered unsteadily, his legs buckling beneath him before he collapsed onto his side. Blood poured through his trembling fingers, staining everything around him crimson.

"Oh God… what have I done?" Viktor whispered, voice breaking as the knife slipped from his trembling grip and clattered harshly to the floor. His knees buckled, and he sank slowly to the ground, eyes locked on the spreading pool of blood that seemed to swallow the light.

"My God!" The words escaped his lips again, voice barely more than a trembling breath as he stared down at the lifeless figure sprawled before him. The deep crimson blood spread like a stain that refused to be wiped away, its metallic tang stinging Viktor's nostrils yet mingling with the suffocating weight of dread in the air.

His legs wavered precariously beneath him, and he staggered backward, voice a barely audible whisper. "Did I… did I kill him?"

Vladimir's harsh, cutting voice shattered the spiral of Viktor's thoughts. "Forget him! We have to get out of here—now!"

Vladimir's face was a grim mess—pale and streaked with blood, his nose broken and bent at a grotesque angle. Still, his movements were urgent and decisive. He snatched the bloodied knife from the floor and slipped it swiftly into his jacket pocket.

"Move! If we stay, we're dead!"

Viktor remained frozen, rooted in place. The sight of the spreading blood and lifeless eyes staring blankly up at the ceiling overwhelmed him, clawing at his resolve. His mind screamed for action, for escape, but his body betrayed him with an oppressive paralysis.

Vladimir did not wait. He grabbed Viktor's arm with a fierce grip, yanking him forcefully toward the door.

"Viktor, now!"

Chapter 7

Viktor sat alone at the kitchen table two days later, the pale light of dawn creeping hesitantly through the thin, worn curtains. The room was silent except for the faint, distant hum of morning traffic outside, yet inside, the oppressive stillness weighed heavily on him, as if the air itself was suffocating. His hands trembled uncontrollably, fingers clutching the crumpled, fragile newspaper so tightly that his knuckles protruded starkly white against his skin. The rough, folded paper scraped and bit into his palms, but Viktor was barely aware of the physical discomfort. His eyes were riveted to the damning headline, the stark black ink clawing its way deeper into his mind with every glance:

"Journalist Found Murdered—Possible Political Motive."

The headline struck him like a heavy blow to the chest, shattering his fragile hope and fracturing any sense of control he thought he had left. This was never supposed to end like this, he thought bitterly, a heavy weight of despair pressing down on his chest. His gaze shifted downward to the victim's photograph printed just beneath the headline. The young man's face was serene and dignified, almost unnervingly peaceful—a heartbreaking contradiction to the brutal violence that had claimed his life during the dark hours of night.

Viktor blinked slowly, struggling to hold back a sudden sting of tears that threatened to spill over, but the tears never came. Instead, an icy knot of dread twisted tighter and tighter in the pit of his stomach. Summoning every ounce of willpower, he forced himself to keep reading. The article revealed more than a simple murder—it sketched a grim tableau of political unrest, shadowed by ruthless suppression. The journalist came from Dagestan, a region fraught with tension, political instability, and simmering violence lurking just beneath the surface. The words hinted at conspiracy, silenced voices, and dangerous secrets—whispers of a deeper, far more perilous truth that no one dared speak aloud.

The question gnawed at Viktor relentlessly, refusing to release its grip on his mind: Why had Vladimir insisted that he carry the knife? The official explanation had always been straightforward and supposedly harmless—the plan was merely to scare the man with a rope, nothing more, nothing deadly. Yet here Viktor was, staring down at the bloody knife still sharp in his hand, its cold metal a bitter reminder of consequences far beyond what he had bargained for. Why had he been given something so lethal? The question cut through him like a jagged shard of broken glass, sharp and unyielding. His hands trembled uncontrollably, and his fists crushed the edges of the newspaper, wrinkling and tearing it further with each squeeze. Each crease in the paper seemed to mirror the cracks fracturing his fragile peace of mind.

The possibility that Vladimir had lied to him from the very beginning clawed at Viktor's thoughts, dark and relentless. Had he been deceived, manipulated into playing a role he never fully understood? Had he been used as a mere pawn in a dangerous political game much larger than himself, one where human lives were expendable? The very idea was almost unbearable—a poison that seeped insidiously into his veins, twisting and corroding his sense of trust and reality.

From across the kitchen table, the normal sounds of family life grated against his already frayed nerves like a cruel and mocking contrast. His sister-in-law's cheerful voice floated through the room, mingling effortlessly with Julia's youthful chatter. Julia, his fifteen-year-old niece, laughed with the carefree innocence only a child untouched by darkness can possess. Their voices were light, filled with warmth and ease, punctuated with spontaneous laughter that seemed to belong to another world altogether.

Viktor felt hopelessly distant from their warmth and simplicity, as though he were imprisoned behind bars forged by his own choices—an invisible, unyielding cage that separated him from the life he once knew and the truths he could no longer face. He sat there quietly, watching them with a hollow ache deep in his chest, yearning to pull himself out of the darkness and step back into a life filled with light, peace, and the fragile normalcy they all took for granted. But the storm raging within him was relentless—dark, fierce, and all-consuming—a swirling whirlwind of guilt, self-doubt, and raw terror that refused to be silenced or ignored. No matter how deeply he longed to join in their laughter and the simple joy they shared, the ever-widening chasm inside him grew wider still, making it impossible to bridge the gap. Viktor was trapped in a shadowed world of isolation, cut off by the unbearable weight of the terrible knowledge he carried and the crushing burden of the man he had become.

Julia's bright, carefree laugh rippled across the room, breaking through the silence that enveloped Viktor like a dense fog. Her laughter, which should have offered some relief or comfort, instead struck him like a hammer against the fragile walls of his resolve. It was a stark reminder of everything he had lost and everything he was no longer allowed to have. She didn't know—Julia, nor his sister-in-law, nor anyone else in the room. None of them had the slightest idea of the nightmare that had unfolded, nor the secret burden Viktor now carried, heavy and raw, like a stone pressing deep into his chest.

Unable to resist, his eyes drifted back to the newspaper article, the black-and-white print blurring slightly as he reread the sentences over and over, as if he could unearth some hidden meaning buried between the lines. The article described Dagestan—a region shrouded in conflict and unrest, nestled precariously next to the volatile lands of Chechnya. It was a place known for political instability, where violence simmered just beneath the surface, ready to erupt at the slightest provocation. Journalists who dared to expose the truth or criticize the government rarely lived long enough to see justice. The unspoken but brutally clear rule was that dissent equated to a death sentence.

A cold shiver ran down Viktor's spine as the grim reality settled deep into his bones—a chilling acknowledgment that he was entangled in something far darker and more dangerous than he had originally imagined. Was Vladimir's plan far more sinister than he had allowed himself to believe? Had Viktor been unwittingly placed on a path toward political assassination, used as a disposable tool in a ruthless game orchestrated by forces beyond his understanding? The thought weighed heavily on him, twisting inside his mind, tightening like a noose around his very being.

The implications gnawed at Viktor's mind like relentless, merciless teeth, chewing away at any semblance of clarity or peace. The questions spiraled endlessly—if Vladimir had deliberately drawn him into a murder with such far-reaching political consequences, what else was buried beneath the surface? What other lies had Vladimir concealed from him, hidden behind carefully constructed masks of trust and loyalty? How deep did this web of deception truly run? The uncertainty clawed at Viktor's sanity, leaving no respite, no moment of calm.

A fierce, burning rage surged through his veins, hot and unrelenting. It coursed through him with a force that threatened to overwhelm, tense and sharp like wildfire. That anger was directed equally toward Vladimir for the betrayal and lies—Vladimir, who had manipulated him and twisted the truth until Viktor no longer knew what was real. It turned inward as well, towards himself, for his blind trust, his weakness in believing what he wanted to believe despite the red flags. And it flickered outward, toward the cruel and indifferent hand fate had dealt him, forcing him into a nightmare he never imagined he'd be part of.

With a trembling hand, Viktor reluctantly pushed the newspaper aside, but the victim's face refused to be dismissed. It lingered persistently, like a ghost haunting the edges of his vision—unyielding, impossible to ignore. The young journalist's calm expression, frozen forever in the coarse black-and-white print, burned into Viktor's memory. He could still hear the haunting sound of the man's gurgling breath, ragged and fading beneath the crushing weight of betrayal and bloodshed. That sound replayed over and over in his mind, an echo he could neither escape nor forget.

Even now, the knife still felt impossibly heavy in his palm, as if the cold steel remembered the terrible, irrevocable purpose it had served. The weight was physical and spiritual—an anchor dragging him deeper into a pit of despair. Viktor closed his eyes tightly, willing the horrific images to dissolve, to vanish into shadow—but the memory refused to relent. The vivid image of blood, the chilling coldness of the blade, and most of all, the last, terrified look in the journalist's eyes—the moment just before death swallowed him whole—played on an endless, torturous loop inside Viktor's heart and mind.

"What have I done?"

The question tore through Viktor's mind like a raw, jagged blade—sharp, agonizing, and impossible to silence. It echoed relentlessly, reverberating through every fiber of his being with a weight that nearly crushed him. The enormity of his actions, the irrevocable consequences, threatened to engulf him completely.

His fists clenched tighter and tighter, nails digging deep, jagged grooves into the flesh of his palms, the sharp pressure burning even as his skin grew raw. The veins along his wrists and forearms stood out stark and pronounced beneath his pale, trembling skin—a physical reflection of the torment raging inside. Despite the searing pain, Viktor could not loosen his grip. It felt as if releasing his fists would mean surrendering to the despair that clutched his soul.

He stole another glance at Julia, her youthful face radiant with innocent joy and laughter. The sight was a cruel and merciless reminder of everything Viktor had lost—the life that could have been, the future forever scarred by the shadow of guilt. The possibility of a simple existence, untainted by sorrow or wrongdoing, seemed impossibly distant now, like a fading dream slipping through his fingers. Her laughter rang in his ears, a painful counterpoint to the turmoil churning in his heart.

But deep down, Viktor knew a bitter truth he could not escape: he wasn't simply running from the law or from the relentless authorities pursuing him. Far worse, he was fleeing from himself—from the torment of his own conscience, the weight of his mistakes, and the ghost of his shattered humanity. The man he once was seemed irretrievably lost, buried beneath the rubble of his actions and choices. His own face, reflected in the cold glass of the window, was a stranger's, haunted and broken.

Around him, the kitchen brightened slowly with the dawn's arrival, the soft hues of morning spilling over the walls and the cluttered table. The world outside moved on, indifferent to the storm of suffering and regret piling like heavy stones inside Viktor's chest. The gentle light held no promise for him, only a stark reminder that life continued even when everything felt shattered.

Viktor remained motionless, frozen in place by the unbearable weight of knowledge pressing down on him. He was trapped—ensnared by a past he had been forced into and could no longer escape. There was no forgiveness waiting for him, no redemption to be found in the shadows of what he had done or what he had become. The path forward stretched out before him, dark and uncertain, littered with the shattered pieces of his own life and the lives of those caught in this tragedy. Every step forward was obscured by loss, pain, and the haunting echoes of a choice that could never be undone.

Chapter 8

Another morning arrived far too early, breaking through the fragile remnants of Viktor's restless night. He rolled out of the narrow, rumpled bed with great effort, his movements slow and heavy, weighed down by fatigue that no amount of sleep seemed to cure. With dragging steps, he made his way to the window, seeking some distraction from the turmoil inside him.

It was mid-July, yet the relentless rain had been pouring for days without mercy, drowning the world in a muted gray haze. The gloomy weather seeped insidiously into his mood, coating his thoughts with a persistent dullness, although deep down Viktor knew that the overcast skies were only a reflection, not the source, of his despondency. What truly haunted him—what gnawed endlessly at his sanity—was the murder of the journalist, a grim shadow that clung to him day and night.

Falling asleep had become an arduous struggle, a steep and painful battle fought every evening. Even when exhaustion eventually claimed him, sleep proved no sanctuary. Instead, it brought with it bizarre and unsettling nightmares—dark dreams that twisted through his mind, relentless and vivid. Each nightmare ended the same way: with Viktor jolting awake, drenched in cold sweat, his heart racing wildly with a terror that refused to dissipate.

At the factory, where he once found at least some semblance of routine, Viktor's patience had completely eroded. Small mistakes that before might have passed unnoticed now seemed unbearable, and he snapped at coworkers with an irritable sharpness that surprised even himself. The tension that coiled tightly within him spilled out in bursts of frustration and anger, though he never fully understood why.

At home, his interactions had dwindled to little more than curt nods and clipped, monosyllabic replies. Communication felt like a distant, exhausting effort. A few nights ago, Natasja had finally gathered the courage to ask if something was wrong, her voice soft and hesitant. Viktor's response was immediate and harsh—a sharp, aggressive "No!" that left her visibly startled and hurt. Since then, she hadn't dared to press the issue. Instead, she directed her worries into something tangible: cooking. She spent long hours in the kitchen, preparing meals she hoped might lift his spirits, clinging to tradition as a balm. Borscht, the hearty, vibrant beet soup with tender chunks of meat and a rich medley of vegetables, simmered gently on the stove—a staple of Russian cuisine, brimming with warmth and comfort.

This morning, Viktor pulled on his clothes with slow, heavy movements before shuffling into the kitchen. The air was thick and rich with the familiar aromas of cabbage and slow-cooked meat, a fragile tether to normalcy in a life unraveling at the edges. The scent filled the room, but no comfort followed; instead, it only deepened the painful contrast between the warmth around him and the cold storm raging within.

Natasja was already at the kitchen counter, her posture slightly hunched with concentration as she methodically prepared golubtsi. With practiced hands, she carefully filled each tender cabbage leaf with a precise mixture of ground meat and rice, her movements slow and deliberate. Later, she would either simmer the stuffed rolls gently in a rich tomato sauce or bake them until tender—a cooking ritual as steady and measured as her quiet attempts to restore a fragile sense of peace in their troubled household. Viktor leaned wearily against the doorway, his eyes fixed on her back, watching the small domestic scene unfold before him. A sharp pang of regret surged through his chest as memories of how harshly he had spoken to her just a few days before flickered in his mind. But the thought of confiding in Natasja was impossible—how could he possibly explain the darkness inside him, the terrible things he had done, or worse, the blood money hidden within the very walls of their home?

His jaw tightened as he bit down hard on his lip, the weight of guilt pressing heavily on his spirit like an unbearable burden. He knew, logically, that the right thing would be to share the money with Natasja and his brother, to be honest and seek some kind of collective future. But even as that thought flickered through his mind, it was extinguished almost immediately. No matter what he decided to do with the money, it would remain his alone, a grim payment for the journalist's death—an unforgivable debt etched in blood.

The cash itself was carefully concealed in an old, battered shoebox, tucked away at the very back of the wardrobe in his bedroom. He had hidden it beneath a disorganized pile of old clothes and worn-out shoes, a secret stash buried so deep it would be all but invisible to anyone casually searching. Viktor was certain that no one else would accidentally stumble upon it, yet every time his thoughts turned to the money, an unmistakable pang of unease crept into his chest, tightening like a vice around his heart. The money was both a curse and a constant reminder—a tangible proof of the price paid for that violent, irreversible act.

As the weeks slowly passed, Viktor found himself gradually pulling away from the suffocating grip of the journalist's murder—a dark shadow that had loomed relentlessly over him. In an effort to reclaim some semblance of normalcy, he joined a local football club with a few friends. On the field, as he chased the ball in a wild, frenzied blur, the weight of his fears and regrets momentarily lifted. For those brief, intense moments, he could forget the dead journalist, the lingering guilt, and Jelena—the woman who had never called him back. Yet, despite his attempts to bury her from his thoughts, Jelena remained at the edges of his mind like a ghost he could neither fully ignore nor dismiss.

Boris Jumashyev, the new owner, seemed to spend far more time in Novgorod than Viktor had first guessed. Boris made frequent visits to the factory, each appearance stirring up a fresh wave of memories and emotions. Every time Viktor saw the man, his thoughts involuntarily drifted to Jelena, flooding him with a yearning both hopeful and painful. He longed to see her again, to hear the familiar sound of her voice, to discover if she had ever thought of him in the weeks since they parted. Though he recognized how futile it was, Viktor often found himself riding his bike back to the park where they had met for the first time, a place now heavy with bittersweet memories. Jelena hadn't reached out, and Viktor had no way of knowing how she was—whether she was well, whether she had recovered from her injury. He wondered if her ankle had truly healed; if it had been broken as he feared, perhaps she was unable to play tennis for months, and her absence that summer would make sense. Still, he clung desperately to a fragile thread of hope, a faint but persistent desire that they might cross paths again someday.

Then, three weeks after the fateful night of the murder, something unexpected happened. Viktor woke up to a sensation almost foreign to him: peace. For the first time in weeks, his sleep had not been shattered by nightmares. He opened his eyes and lazily glanced over at the clock sitting on the bedside table—it was already nine in the morning. It was Sunday, and warm sunlight spilled generously through the window, bathing his room in a soft, golden glow. Viktor rose from bed and moved over to the window, throwing it open wide to welcome the crisp morning air. Outside, the distant, joyful laughter of children playing between the apartment blocks filtered up to him—a simple, pure sound that cut through the weight of his thoughts.

He paused, savoring the moment, the feeling of quiet calm settling over him like a balm he hadn't realized he needed. A perfect day for a bike ride, he thought, a faint flicker of genuine anticipation kindling inside him. For the first time in a long while, the future didn't seem so bleak, and the possibility of something good—something ordinary— stirred quietly in the depths of his heart.

As he cycled into the park, Viktor's heart skipped an unexpected beat, jolted by a sudden, sharp pang of recognition and longing. There she was—Jelena—seated gracefully on a worn wooden bench nestled inside one of the tennis courts. Around her stood two teenagers, a girl and a boy close to her age; their voices entwined in lighthearted conversation, punctuated by bursts of laughter that floated softly across the court. Near her, a blond-haired young man sat with an unmistakable aura of confidence, his easy poise causing Viktor's stomach to tighten with a sharp twist of envy and unease. Together, they formed an image of effortless joy and carefree privilege—a stark, almost painful contrast to the shadowed reality of Viktor's own fractured and burdened life.

Slowly, Jelena rose from the bench, her movement fluid and natural. She glanced in Viktor's direction, and for a fleeting, fragile moment, Viktor dared to believe she had recognized him—perhaps even that she might rise to greet him. His chest tightened again, this time with a surge of hopeful anticipation that felt both exhilarating and fragile. But instead of approaching, she shrugged off her jacket with a casual motion and turned her attention to the yellow tennis ball in her hand. With quick, rhythmic strokes, she began bouncing the ball, her racket deftly guiding its arc between the ground and her grip, each bounce light and precise. Her movements were smooth and effortless; it was clear her ankle had fully healed, ready to carry her across the court with the grace of a seasoned player.

The blond-haired man stood and moved to her side. Together, they walked to the far edge of the court, assuming positions as if preparing for a match. Viktor's gaze lingered on the young man, a sharp wave of jealousy twisting painfully in his chest. Who was this confident stranger—her boyfriend, perhaps? Questions swirled through Viktor's mind, but his body remained frozen, paralyzed by indecision and doubt. Should he approach her? Say something? Yet what words could possibly bridge the vast, yawning chasm that had grown between them? Viktor shook his head, chastising himself quietly, feeling foolish and helpless in equal measure. Still, he stayed rooted to the spot, unable or unwilling to tear his eyes away from her.

As the match began, Jelena's laughter rang out—light, bright, carefree—as she flitted effortlessly across the court, each movement radiating a vitality that seemed completely untouchable. Seeing her so radiant, so alive and distant, Viktor made a quiet, painful decision. He mounted his bike once more and pedaled away slowly, the sound of her laughter echoing relentlessly in his mind—a vivid, piercing reminder of the vast, unreachable world that she inhabited, a world forever closed off to him.

Without any particular destination in mind, Viktor allowed his legs to guide him aimlessly through the winding streets of Novgorod. His thoughts spun wildly, tangled and chaotic, as the city's ancient heartbeat pulsed around him. Novgorod—a city steeped in over eleven centuries of history—felt alive to him in a way that transcended its present struggles. Its medieval churches rose proudly like silent guardians, stoic sentinels preserving memories of a time long past. These sacred landmarks had somehow withstood the devastating purges of the Soviet regime, a cruel and calculated effort to erase religion and heritage. Whereas so many other cities had lost their sacred monuments to demolition crews and neglect, Novgorod had fought to cling to its roots—maintaining over forty ancient sanctuaries in all, a miracle and testament to resilience in the face of erasure. As Viktor cycled past the towering, weathered spires, he felt a flicker of awe mixed with melancholy—an echo of endurance and survival that contrasted sharply with the fragile state of his own life.

As Viktor weaved carefully through the narrow, cobbled streets of Novgorod, memories from his childhood surfaced unbidden, reflections ingrained by the rigid lessons about communism he had been taught. The Party had drilled into him that faith was nothing more than a relic of the past—an old superstition best discarded. The only truths that mattered were concrete and immediate: this life, this fleeting moment, and then the silence of death that followed. The cold finality of that teaching chilled him to his core. Death felt brutally absolute, a closing door from which there was no return.

Yet, beneath the surface of those hardened beliefs, a deeper yearning lingered inside Viktor—an almost desperate hunger for something more meaningful, something eternal and beyond the grasp of mortal understanding. A God, perhaps. Redemption. Forgiveness. But that hope now collided painfully with the crushing weight of his guilt. Since that dreadful night, everything had changed irrevocably. He had taken a life—another human being's life. Could forgiveness ever find its way to someone like him? Could he ever be worthy of it?

A small, stubborn part of Viktor clung to the grim comfort of the Party's teachings; if nothing waited beyond death, then perhaps judgment was nothing to fear. Maybe after his final breath, all his sins would simply vanish into nothingness. But then, another, more terrifying thought whispered through his mind—what if they were wrong? What if God did exist, watching, judging, waiting for him to answer for what he had done? The possibility unsettled him more than he cared to admit.

Eventually, his wandering brought him to the gates of Novgorod's Kremlin, its ancient, towering walls casting long, somber shadows across the wide cobblestone square. Viktor dismounted his bike, the crunch of its tires against the uneven stones breaking the heavy stillness that hung in the air. The Kremlin's grandeur was undeniable—a stark reminder of Russia's rich, enduring legacy. On most days, the sight left him in quiet awe, a connection to something larger than himself. But today, instead of awe, the mighty ramparts and ornate towers deepened the oppressive weight in his chest, a crushing reminder of the world he had become trapped within.

Pushing his bike across the broad, echoing square, Viktor's breath suddenly caught in his throat. Ahead of him, a figure in a crisp uniform appeared—a policeman. The sudden presence of law and order sent a cold wave of panic crashing down his spine, breaking out in a clammy sweat. His legs felt leaden and unsteady, but he forced himself to continue moving, swallowing the rising tide of fear and trying to steady his trembling breath. Had they found him out? Did they already know the terrible secret he carried—what he had done?

The officer walked with quiet purpose, the sharp, steady thud of his boots striking the cobblestones loud and unnervingly precise in Viktor's ears. His mind raced uncontrollably, panic swirling in his chest, threatening to overwhelm his carefully maintained composure. Desperately, Viktor averted his gaze and cast it toward one of the restored Kremlin buildings, pretending to be absorbed in the intricate architectural details carved into its ancient stones. But his hands betrayed him, trembling visibly as he gripped the bike's handlebars.

The distance between them was closing rapidly with every measured step of the policeman. Viktor's heart pounded so loud it seemed to drown out all other sound, each beat threatening to give away his fear. Then, with a sudden, sharp stop, the policeman stood just meters away from him. Viktor braced himself for the worst, the weight of dread settling like a stone in his gut as he held his breath, waiting for what was to come.

"Viktor?" The voice was warm and familiar, cutting sharply through his tense thoughts and startling him out of his fearful trance. "It's been ages!"

Viktor blinked, his apprehension momentarily dissolving into confusion. There was something unmistakably familiar about that voice, a fragment from a long-buried past. As the officer's face broke into a broad grin, recognition flickered through Viktor's mind like a flash of lightning.

"Don't tell me you don't recognize me," Ivan teased, amusement dancing in his eyes.

"I… I…" Viktor stammered, his gaze fixed on the man's face as the pieces fell into place. Recognition dawned fully. "Ivan?" he breathed, the tension in his shoulders loosening ever so slightly. "So, you really did become a policeman?"

Ivan laughed, the sound hearty, genuine, and infectious. "I did! Remember how I wouldn't shut up about it back then? All those times I said I'd join the force? And you? Did you ever make it big like you claimed you would?"

Viktor forced a half-hearted smile, though unease simmered beneath the surface, untouched by the momentary camaraderie. "Not exactly. A rich man doesn't bike around town like this, does he?" he replied, brushing off the question with a hint of self-deprecation.

Ivan stepped closer, his large frame towering over Viktor as he clapped a firm, friendly hand on his shoulder. Yet beneath the warmth of the gesture, there was an intensity in Ivan's gaze that Viktor couldn't shake—something serious, weighty, lurking just beneath the friendly façade.

"Listen," Ivan said, lowering his voice into a conspiratorial tone, "I might have a little side gig for you. Pays well. Interested?"

The air between them thickened, heavy with unspoken implications. Viktor's mind churned with rising unease, but also a flicker of curiosity edged his caution. He hesitated before replying, his voice tentative.

"What kind of job?" he asked, wary yet intrigued.

Ivan leaned in, a sly grin widening across his face. "Nothing too complicated. Just a favor… for an old friend."

"Are you serious? Me, a bodyguard?" Viktor's voice wavered between incredulity and nervous laughter. The idea seemed absurd—a striking departure from his current aimless existence—yet, beneath the surface, the proposition sparked an undeniable flicker of interest.

Ivan's smirk deepened, unwavering. "Dead serious. It's good money, Viktor. And you've got what it takes. Remember the factory incident? Those thugs tried to muscle in, and you reacted faster and smarter than most trained cops would. You've got instincts—that's what people pay for."

Viktor glanced away, heat rising to his face under Ivan's steady, evaluating gaze. "I just… reacted," he muttered, unsure if his response belied skill or mere luck.

"And that's precisely why you're perfect for this job," Ivan pressed on, his tone low and persuasive. "It's not about posing like you're tough—it's about acting when it counts. You've already proven you can do that when it really mattered."

Then Ivan dropped the name that made Viktor's stomach clench like a fist. "The gig's for Boris Jumashyev."

The words hit Viktor like a sudden punch to the gut. "Jumashyev? The factory owner?" His voice barely concealed a mixture of surprise and apprehension.

"Exactly," Ivan confirmed with a grin. "He's always looking for reliable security. These wealthy types—they're paranoid for good reason."

Viktor's brow furrowed deeply as his thoughts tangled in doubt, curiosity, and something he couldn't quite name. "And you think I can just step into that world?"

Ivan clapped him firmly on the shoulder, confidence radiating from every ounce of his being. "Not think, Viktor. I know. The question is—do you?"

Chapter 9

The night air was cool and crisp, carrying the faint rustle of leaves and the distant hum of laughter. The garden sprawled before Viktor, bathed in the gentle glow of hundreds of soft, golden fairy lights that twinkled like stars caught amidst the late-summer blooms. Each delicate flower seemed to shimmer in the luminance, petals kissed by the soft light and the lingering scent of earth warmed by the day. Viktor straightened with a subtle adjustment to the stiff collar of his impeccably tailored suit, the fabric unfamiliar against his skin. This new uniform, pristine and heavy with expectation, heightened the knot of unease tightening in his gut. Tonight marked his inaugural shift as a bodyguard for Boris Jumashyev—an assignment that carried weight far beyond the polished veneer of the lavish event.

Beneath his jacket, the reassuring but sobering presence of a concealed 9mm pistol pressed lightly against his ribs, a constant reminder of the gravity and potential danger encircling him. The mansion behind him was alive with activity, the grand dining hall spilling its ambiance of luxury and merriment into the night air. Muffled laughter, the clinking of crystal glasses, and muted conversations wove together into a symphony of upper-class festivity. A soft breeze meandered through the garden, carrying with it a delicate mixture of blooming roses and the fresh scent of damp earth, though Viktor was too wound tight with tension to savor the peacefulness.

A sudden crackle buzzed in his earpiece, pulling him sharply out of his momentary trance. "Guests are moving to the outdoor tent," a voice instructed quietly but firmly.

Acknowledging the command with a swift nod, Viktor's gaze flicked carefully over the garden shadows. His eyes, sharp and vigilant, traced each movement—waiting, calculating—and then he moved toward the terrace with purposeful steps. The party tent stood out like a glowing beacon in the darkness, its spacious interior bathed in a soft, inviting light that pooled over the freshly watered grass. Viktor positioned himself at the corner of the house, choosing a spot that offered a clear vantage point, overseeing both the terrace and the main entrance to the tent. Every sense was alert, every muscle primed for action.

And then he saw him—a figure who did not belong, yet seemed expertly woven into the scene. Among the well-dressed guests and attentive waitstaff moving seamlessly between conversations and clinking glasses, one man stood out with unsettling subtlety. He carried a tray like the others, but his movements were too smooth, too calculated, betraying a practiced ease that felt out of place. Viktor's instincts flared sharply, an alarm bell ringing in his mind. He fixed his eyes on the man, silent and unassuming, and began to tail him discreetly through the shimmering crowd.

The moment unfolded with startling swiftness. The man stopped beside a woman adorned in an extravagant diamond necklace, the gems sparkling ostentatiously under the party lights. With a charming, disarming smile and a quick, subtle motion that went unnoticed by the woman engrossed in conversation, the man deftly slipped the necklace free.

Viktor's pulse throttled upward in response, watching as the necklace vanished into the man's pocket with an ease that spoke of long practice. His hand twitched near the hidden firearm at his side, ready—but he restrained himself. This was no time to act impulsively; the situation demanded patience and precision.

Instead, Viktor followed the thief with measured steps and unwavering focus. The man wove expertly through the tent, his tray balanced effortlessly, eyes scanning, searching for the next mark as though he were hunting. Viktor's mind raced, weighing every possible move, every consequence, calculating the safest and most effective way to intercept without endangering the guests or tipping off the thief prematurely. The night had shifted, and the quiet tension of the garden party now pulsed with dangerous promise.

The flickering lights of the party cast shimmering reflections off the thief's pocket, where the stolen diamond necklace now nestled like a hidden treasure. Viktor felt a tight coil of tension twist in his chest, his instincts flaring fiercely, urging him toward immediate action. Every fiber of his being screamed to move, to intervene—but when? And how?

His fingers instinctively brushed the cold metal of the pistol concealed beneath his jacket—the reassuring, unyielding weight grounding him amid the swirling chaos. The night's deceptive serenity masked the danger threading its way through the celebration, and Viktor understood one thing clearly: he could not, would not, allow the man to slip away. Not tonight.

He pushed decisively through the milling crowd, muscles coiling with adrenaline, heart hammering against his ribs. The startled faces of guests blurred past, their murmurs and the delicate clinking of glasses dissolving into a distant background noise beneath his razor-sharp focus. Each step brought him closer to the thief.

Ahead, the man suddenly turned, his eyes locking with Viktor's for a fleeting, electric moment—a shared recognition of the game that had unfolded. At that instant, the tray in the thief's hands clattered to the marble floor, silverware scattering in a chaotic scatter beneath the gasps and startled shouts of the crowd. In that heartbeat, the man bolted, a flash of motion disappearing toward the open door that led back inside the mansion.

"Stop him!" Viktor's sharp command cut through the stunned silence like a whip crack. He didn't wait to see if anyone responded—he launched himself forward, weaving fluidly between frozen guests, dodging grasping hands and scattered chairs.

The thief vanished into the mansion's interior, swallowed by the grand structure. Viktor's chest tightened, adrenaline igniting his legs as he surged after the fleeing figure without hesitation.

"Where did he go?!" a fellow guard called breathlessly, closing in on Viktor's side.

"We split up!" Viktor barked back, his voice crisp and commanding. "You take the first floor—we'll sweep the upper levels!" Without missing a beat, Viktor was already racing up the grand staircase two steps at a time, adrenaline sharpening his senses.

The second floor stretched out before him—a disorienting labyrinth of shadow-strewn hallways, closed doors, and hidden corners. Viktor's unfamiliarity with the layout gnawed at his resolve, each second dragging endlessly as he stormed from one door to the next, flinging them open in rapid succession. The first room was empty; the second, a cluttered storage closet. Frustration prickled beneath his skin with every fruitless search.

Then, through the ambient noise, a subtle sound caught his sharp attention—a faint but unmistakable creak. Viktor froze, breath catching in his throat, straining to listen. There it was again: the unmistakable sound of a window sliding open against the cool night air.

Without hesitation, he sprinted toward the far end of the hallway, heart pounding in sync with his pounding footsteps. His hands trembled slightly as he reached for the handle of the last door, wrenching it open.

There, framed against the dim glow of the night, stood the thief—halfway out of the window, a dark coil of fire escape rope slung over the ledge below. The man was poised for escape, the cool night air tugging at his coat.

"Stop!" Viktor shouted, his voice raw, urgent, and hoarse from the chase. Every fiber of his body screamed for the moment to freeze—to end this pursuit once and for all.

The thief didn't hesitate for a single moment. With the practiced ease of someone who had done this many times before, he seized the rough rope of the fire escape and began his descent down the side of the mansion. Each movement was fluid, controlled, and relentless as he made his escape into the night. Viktor's mind raced—there was no time to hesitate. He couldn't allow the man to vanish into the shadows, to slip through his grasp like smoke.

Without a second thought, Viktor lunged for the rope, gripping it firmly and swinging himself out after the fleeing figure. The coarse fibers bit sharply into his palms, the sting mingling with the rush of adrenaline as he slid downward. The night air whipped past him, crisp and unforgiving against his face, heightening every sense. When his boots finally hit the uneven ground below, they landed with a thud that jarred his knees, briefly buckling them before he steadied himself.

Ahead, the thief's dark silhouette was already darting toward the parking lot, moving with the desperate swiftness of a man driven by fear and determination. Gravel crunched noisily under his hurried steps, each sound pounding in Viktor's ears.

His own boots thundered against the hard ground, matching pace as he pushed himself harder, lungs burning with short, sharp gasps of breath. The thief was fast—too fast—but Viktor was fueled by unwavering determination. Without hesitation, he veered off the path, cutting a line across the wet lawn. The damp grass offered little traction, and suddenly his foot caught among the cruel arms of a rosebush. Sharp thorns tore into his trousers and grazed his skin, sending a sting that drove a brief wince through him, but he didn't falter. Not now.

As the parking lot floodlights flickered on, their harsh beams cutting through the darkness, they illuminated the thief in stark relief against the cars. Viktor's chest tightened painfully. Despite his effort, it was clear he wouldn't catch the man before he reached the fleet of vehicles. The moment had arrived—the only choice left.

He skidded to an abrupt halt, his boots grinding against the gravel. In one fluid, practiced motion, he drew his pistol and raised it, heart hammering in his chest like a drum. His breath steadied as best he could, muscles taut, finger poised on the trigger.

"Don't miss," he muttered quietly, more to himself than anyone else.

The gunshot cracked through the still night air—sharp, final, echoing against the nearby walls. The thief emitted a strangled cry, clutching his shoulder as the pain toppled him to the ground. Viktor didn't hesitate. He sprinted forward and planted his boot firmly on the man's injured arm, ensuring he couldn't escape or resist.

"Not so fast," Viktor growled, voice low and unforgiving. Catching his breath, he knelt down beside the fallen thief and rifled through his pockets with rapid, practiced fingers. His hand closed around something cool and solid. Pulling it into the light, he found a diamond necklace glittering maliciously under the artificial glow—a prize stolen moments before. Then another. And then another. The haul was staggering.

"Damn," Viktor muttered, breath hitching as he stared, disbelief mixing with grim realization. This wasn't a one-time petty thief—this was a seasoned professional, and the evidence was damning.

The next morning, Viktor stood in the security chief's office, the air thick with unspoken judgment and terse expectation. The atmosphere was as cold and unwelcoming as the steel-gray walls curtaining the room. Between them, the imposing desk loomed like a barrier, a silent emblem of authority and scrutiny. Viktor's fingers gripped the edge of his chair with a subtle tension, knuckles white from the effort as he fought to mask the anxious energy simmering beneath his carefully composed exterior.

The chief's voice cut through the heavy silence, low and deliberate, each word carefully measured yet laden with an unmistakable demand for complete and unvarnished honesty. His piercing eyes locked onto Viktor with an intensity that felt almost predatory—sharp, unyielding, impossible to evade.

"Tell me everything," he commanded, his tone brooking no argument.

Viktor swallowed hard, the knot in his throat tightening as the flood of memories surged back with vivid clarity. His words spilled out in a rapid, tense rush, the adrenaline of the previous night still humming just beneath the surface of his voice. He painted a detailed picture—the sudden, jarring sound of the tray crashing against the marble floor; the blur of the thief vanishing into the gloom; the fierce, breathless chase that followed as his heart pounded like a war drum;

and the agonizing moment when he made the split-second decision to draw his weapon.

As he recounted the sharp crack of the gunshot and the thief collapsing to the ground, his voice faltered slightly, betraying the lingering echo of that moment in his mind. The memory of startled gasps from the guests, the flashing floodlights illuminating the tense scene, reverberated through his thoughts as if the night's events were still unfolding around him.

When Viktor finally stopped speaking, the room dipped back into a weighty silence, heavy and suffocating. The chief steepled his fingers under his chin, his gaze never wavering from Viktor's face. Like a hawk fixated on its prey, he studied every nuance, reading between the lines of what had been said and unsaid.

After a long pause, he broke the silence, his voice quieter but no less commanding: "What's your regular job?"

The unexpected question caught Viktor off guard. He hesitated, a sudden flush of embarrassment creeping up his neck and warming his face. For a moment, the grand responsibility of his current role seemed miles away from the truth of his everyday life.

"I... work at the fertilizer plant," he admitted softly, his voice barely above a murmur, as if the words themselves felt out of place in this austere office.

The chief raised a single eyebrow, a flicker of surprise briefly softening his otherwise stoic and imposing demeanor.

"The fertilizer plant?" he repeated slowly, skepticism threading through his tone as if questioning how those two worlds—Viktor's ordinary livelihood and the elite security role he was now tasked with—could possibly align. "Then how did you end up working security for an event like this?"

The question hung heavily in the air, laden with implicit judgment and curiosity. Viktor shifted uncomfortably in his chair, feeling the weight of scrutiny pressing down on him like an invisible force. Yet despite the unease, he answered candidly, recounting the unexpected twist of fate that had steered him here—a police friend who had vouched for him after witnessing his courageous actions earlier that summer.

It was a small act of faith from an unlikely ally, but it had opened a door to this world of glittering mansions and hidden dangers, of high-stakes protection and sharp-edged vigilance. And now, standing at the crossroads between who he was and who he might become, Viktor listened closely to the chief's next words, knowing this moment could define the path ahead.

Viktor recounted the harrowing day when armed gangsters had stormed the fertilizer plant—a day that had tested not only his courage but his very resolve. He spoke of how, despite being outnumbered and facing overwhelming danger, he had stood his ground. His unwavering stance had not only protected his coworkers but had also earned him the quiet respect of those around him, as well as a fleeting moment of recognition in the local newspapers. The headlines had painted him as a reluctant hero, a man who had risen unexpectedly to face chaos head-on.

As Viktor spoke, the chief's eyes narrowed, focusing intently on the story unfolding before him. A subtle flicker of something—perhaps admiration or begrudging respect—briefly lit his gaze, betraying the otherwise impassive exterior.

"Ah," the chief finally murmured, his tone thoughtful and measured. "That was you? I remember reading about that incident. Quite the story."

Viktor gave a slight nod, feeling his chest tighten with a mixture of hope and apprehension as he awaited the verdict he so desperately wanted to hear. The silence stretched between them just long enough for the question that had been forming on his lips to escape.

"Do you think... you'll hire me again?" His voice carried the faintest edge of eagerness, betraying the guarded optimism buried beneath his calm exterior.

The chief's lips curled into a faint, enigmatic smile as he leaned back in his chair, which creaked softly under his weight. For a moment, Viktor thought he detected a glimmer of approval flickering in the man's eyes, a silent nod of recognition for the determination he had shown. Then, with deliberate slowness, the chief delivered his response—a single, maddeningly ambiguous word.

"Maybe."

It was neither the firm affirmation Viktor had longed for nor a definitive rejection. The word lingered in the air, heavy with both possibility and doubt, leaving Viktor caught between cautious hope and simmering uncertainty.

His chest grew heavier as the chief turned his attention away from him, focusing instead on the scattered papers and reports lying on the desk before him. The subtle shift in posture signaled the meeting's end, leaving Viktor to process the unresolved verdict and the uncertain path that lay ahead.

Chapter 10

Viktor cast a wary, skeptical glance at the sour-faced foreman. Rumors had been circulating among the workers like wildfire—whispers that management was planning a sweeping downsizing, targeting older employees they deemed less productive or expendable. While Viktor had convinced himself the rumors didn't apply to him, a faint flicker of unease gnawed quietly at the edges of his mind, refusing to be ignored.

"What's this about?" he asked cautiously, brushing the sweat from his brow as the late-morning heat pressed down. "My shift's almost over—I was just about to head home."

Sergei's scowl deepened, his face tightening with displeasure. "How should I know? You've been ordered to report to the director's office. No explanations."

Viktor frowned and nodded, trying to mask the sudden spike of tension in his chest as he turned away from the foreman and made his way toward the director's office. Outside the heavy wooden door, his hand hovered uncertainly above the polished brass handle, the faint echo of his heartbeat loud in the quiet hallway. Taking a deep, steadying breath to calm the rise of anxiety within him, he pressed down on the latch and slowly pushed the door open.

Inside, the factory director sat behind a desk that loomed like a throne of authority. Neatly arranged papers lay spread before him, their corners sharp and precise, a polished nameplate gleaming coldly beneath the overhead light. The room was large and austere, the muted colors and sparse decoration lending a stark formality to the setting.

"Come in," the director said curtly, gesturing toward the lone chair positioned across from him.

Viktor stepped inside, the soft creak of his boots against the worn floorboards echoing slightly in the tense silence. The room wasn't empty. Three men stood near the tall windows, their figures casting sharp silhouettes against the pale glow of the morning light flooding the space. One figure immediately drew Viktor's attention—Boris Jumashyev. The oligarch stood with his back turned, gazing out at the sprawling factory grounds beyond the glass, his posture rigid and commanding.

What was Jumashyev doing here? Viktor's unease prickled sharply up his spine, a subtle warning that this meeting was far from ordinary.

Breaking the silence, a blonde man—someone Viktor didn't recognize—spoke first. His voice was calm and measured but carried an unmistakable edge of authority, every word deliberate and precise.

"Thanks for coming in so quickly," the man began, locking Viktor with a piercing gaze that felt less like an invitation and more like an evaluation, as if weighing him against an unseen scale. "Let's get straight to the point. You were—"

Suddenly, Boris Jumashyev turned around, and the atmosphere in the room shifted palpably, thickening with an almost tangible intensity. The blonde man stopped mid-sentence, silence falling under the weight of Jumashyev's imposing presence. The room seemed to contract around the oligarch, his powerful aura drawing every pair of eyes like a magnetic force.

Viktor felt those penetrating, dark eyes sweep over him, scrutinizing every detail of his appearance and posture, as though searching for truths even he wasn't fully aware of. The mounting tension stretched taut until finally, Jumashyev's lips curved into a slow, deliberate smile.

This was no casual, polite gesture—this smile radiated power, approval, and silent command. It was the kind of smile that could change a man's fate with a simple expression.

"The way you handled the jewelry thief," Jumashyev began, his tone even and measured, deliberate in every syllable, "was impressive. I have many enemies. Men in my position always do."

Boris Jumashyev paused deliberately, the weight of his words hanging heavy in the air between them. "That means I must protect myself, my family, and my interests," he said slowly, each syllable underscored with unspoken threats and the heavy responsibility that came with his position.

Viktor held his breath, the room seeming to shrink around them as Jumashyev's eyes bore into him with sharp precision. The oligarch's voice cut through the silence, crisp and exact. "I've just learned you work here, at my factory," he said, the acknowledgment seeming almost incidental yet laced with importance. "I need a bodyguard—someone quick-thinking, independent. Someone who doesn't flinch under pressure. You strike me as that man."

A surge of adrenaline coursed through Viktor's veins. His heart thundered so loudly he was certain Jumashyev could hear it. The weight of the moment crashed over him, bringing with it disbelief mingled with cautious hope. Could this actually be happening? Was this offer real?

"Are you offering me a permanent position as your bodyguard?" Viktor asked, his voice calm and steady despite the storm of emotions swirling beneath the surface. The question hung in the air, a fragile thread connecting two very different worlds.

Jumashyev stepped forward, his commanding presence filling the room. Standing directly before Viktor, the space between them charged with authority, his gaze locked on Viktor with unyielding intensity. "Are you interested?" he asked, his tone blending a sharp challenge with a subtle invitation—an unspoken test of resolve and courage.

Without hesitation, Viktor shot to his feet, the chair scraping lightly against the floorboards. He reached out and gripped Jumashyev's outstretched hand firmly, feeling the strength and certainty in the oligarch's grasp. "Absolutely," he said, his voice brimming with conviction, sincerity shining through. "I'm very interested."

From a young age, Viktor had heard the saying that small men often carried great impatience, and he wasn't surprised when Jumashyev declared that he would start immediately. There was no grace period, no time for second-guessing or deliberation. The offer wasn't just made—it was a command, an expectation to rise at once to the challenge.

Though Viktor didn't hesitate, a shadow of uncertainty flickered in the back of his mind. What does being a full-time bodyguard truly entail? The responsibilities, the dangers, the sacrifices—it all felt distant and vague, yet undeniably real. He pushed those doubts aside, resolving firmly: I'll figure it out as I go.

By the time evening settled over the city, the stakes of Viktor's new role had become painfully clear. Boris Jumashyev had a critical meeting scheduled in Moscow the very next morning, an event that demanded his full attention and utmost protection. Viktor would accompany him on this journey—his first real test as the man entrusted with guarding an oligarch's life.

His path as Jumashyev's bodyguard, fraught with peril and uncertainty, would begin before the first light of dawn. The quiet garden parties and factory floors of the past were already fading into memory, replaced by a world where vigilance and resolve would be his daily currency.

Chapter 11

The next morning, as the engines of the private jet roared to life beneath him, Viktor sat quietly by the window, his gaze fixed on the ever-shrinking landscape below. Novgorod—the familiar, muted world he had known all his life—was receding fast, replaced by a vast and imposing horizon. Ahead lay the sprawling capital: Moscow, a giant both magnificent and daunting. He adjusted the stiff lapels of his suit jacket, the fabric crisp and unfamiliar against his skin, and took a slow, deliberate breath, bracing himself for whatever awaited. Whatever challenges and dangers lay ahead, Viktor silently vowed that he would meet them head-on, ready for the demands of this new life.

The days that followed unfurled like a vivid dream—each moment surreal and overwhelming in equal measure. Trailing closely behind Boris Jumashyev, Viktor moved cautiously but with growing eagerness, absorbing every detail of the life he had stepped into. This was a world utterly unlike the monotonous, predictable grind of his old existence in Novgorod. Moscow, with its grandeur and relentless energy, felt like an entirely different realm. The city's skyline was a breathtaking contradiction: gleaming glass skyscrapers pierced the sky with modern ambition, standing shoulder to shoulder with centuries-old stone facades whose weathered surfaces whispered silent stories of a bygone era. The stark collision of past and present left Viktor both awestruck and overwhelmed—as if caught between two powerful currents pulling him in opposite directions.

For the first time in his life, Viktor found himself standing inside the Kremlin—the very heart of Russian power and history. The massive fortress walls burned a vivid red beneath the sunlight, golden onion domes shimmered brilliantly, and intricately designed churches rose like jewels against the sky. He was left utterly speechless, the grandeur and weight of the place surpassing everything he had imagined. He recalled the old saying he had heard so many times:

"Over Moscow lies only the Kremlin, and over the Kremlin lies only God."

Now, standing in the shadow of those age-old walls, the truth of those words permeated him deeply. The grandeur was intoxicating yet humbling, awe-inspiring yet intimidating. He felt like an outsider—someone whose very presence might somehow disturb the sacredness of the place. It was a reminder of just how far he had come, but also how vast the gulf was between his humble origins and the world he now inhabited.

Later, riding through the city in a sleek limousine, Viktor watched Moscow's sprawling panorama unfold like a cinematic reel. Wide, majestic boulevards swept past beneath towering monuments, while narrow cobblestone streets wove between lush green parks and historic buildings. His eyes lingered on Red Square, its vast open expanse illuminated against the darkening sky, the glowing outlines of St. Basil's Cathedral and the Kremlin walls burning into his memory. The sight nearly stole his breath, and he fought to steady himself, refusing to gape like a starstruck boy. Every corner of this city seemed to pulse with stories—tales of revolution, of triumph, of power wrested and wielded across centuries. Moscow was alive with history and raw energy, a living testament to a nation that had been shaped by destiny, challenge, and unyielding will.

At night, alone in his modest hotel room, Viktor sat hunched over a newly purchased, large map of Moscow spread out before him on the desk. His fingers traced the intricate web of streets, boulevards, and squares, each winding line pulling him deeper into the city's vast and tangled mysteries. For a man who had rarely ventured beyond the quiet, predictable confines of Novgorod, Moscow was an overwhelming enigma—alive with possibility yet saturated in unspoken rules and hidden dangers. Though the city dazzled with its shimmering lights and relentless activity, Viktor couldn't shake the gnawing feeling that he didn't quite belong. The polished luxury cars that cruised past, the high-end restaurants where deals were struck over fine wine, and the opulent surroundings felt like a borrowed dream—one that could unravel at any moment. He feared that one wrong step might shatter the fragile illusion and wake him from this gilded world he had been thrust into.

Earlier, sitting in the front seat of the sleek limousine, Viktor had strained to catch snippets of Boris Jumashyev's conversation from the subdued, plush cabin behind him. Words like "negotiation," "shareholders," and "stakeholders" floated toward him, heavy with significance and authority. Though many of the terms eluded his full understanding, the tone was unmistakable—this was a world governed by high stakes and carefully calculated power plays. Every sentence was loaded with consequence, every pause brimming with unspoken strategy.

Beside Boris sat a man whose impeccably tailored suit and thick cigar clenched firmly between his teeth painted a picture of influence and command. Thin wisps of blue-gray smoke curled lazily into the air as he spoke in low, deliberate tones. Viktor felt profoundly out of place—as if intruding on a realm he barely comprehended, a silent observer to a sophisticated dance of power and persuasion. His eyes involuntarily flicked toward Boris, who exuded an aura of calm confidence; the very presence of the oligarch commanded respect and attention.

In stark contrast, Viktor's own self-image was sharply at odds with this world. He felt like an imposter—a man plucked from obscurity and thrust into the glaring spotlight of untouchable wealth and influence. What if they saw through the façade? What if this gleaming, gilded reality crumbled the moment someone realized that beneath the polished surface, he was still the man from a small industrial town? The thought gnawed at him relentlessly, yet he kept his face neutral, his hands resting tensely on his knees, hiding the turmoil beneath.

As the limousine glided smoothly through the sprawling city streets, Viktor gazed out at the metropolis unfurling before him—the glittering skyline, historic landmarks, and bustling crowds—trying to silence the whispering doubts in his mind. He may not have been born into this rarefied world, but for now, he was part of it. And with every fiber of his being, he resolved to prove he belonged—no matter the cost.

The conversation inside the limousine's dimly lit cabin carried a weight that seemed to overshadow Moscow's shimmering grandeur outside. Viktor sat tensely in the front passenger seat, his eyes fixed ahead on the glistening streets, but his ears relentlessly attuned to every word drifting back.

"It feels like an eternity since President Boris Yeltsin and his protégé, Yegor Gaidar, first came to power," Boris began, his voice steady and measured, touched with a hint of nostalgia.

"That was December 1991, wasn't it?" Rybkin replied, his tone carrying a practiced cheerfulness that belied the gravity beneath the conversation.

Boris nodded thoughtfully. "Yes. It's strange to reflect on how weakened the Russian state was back then—unable to perform even its most basic functions. The upheaval, the uncertainty… it was a time when everything seemed to hang in the balance."

Viktor listened, absorbing the weight of history in their words—a past shaped by revolution and chaos, a nation struggling to find its footing in the new world order. The city outside, with its powerful monuments and vibrant life, was a living testament to that turbulent legacy.

"But that weakness was our opportunity," Rybkin interjected with a low, unsettling laugh that seemed to carry both triumph and cynicism. "Communism was gasping its final breath. Gorbachev was forced out of the Kremlin, and Yeltsin stepped in as president. That upheaval—it ignited something in me, a chance I couldn't ignore. It was then I started my computer sales cooperative."

Boris's eyes glimmered with a faint, calculated smile as he added, "A business you kindly let me buy into."

Rybkin chuckled, the sound rich and knowing. "That's right—and together, we transformed that small cooperative into a private bank."

Boris's voice took on a lower, more reflective tone as he continued, "And to think, the government actually entrusted our bank with managing state funds and distributing loans to businesses and regions. Inflation was running rampant—thirty percent, sometimes even forty—and we made fortunes simply by delaying payments by a few days. The high interest rates practically minted money for us."

"An unbelievable stroke of luck," Rybkin agreed, exhaling a swirling cloud of cigar smoke that hung heavy in the cabin's subdued light. "The bureaucracy was oblivious to the scale of the profits we were quietly reaping."

Boris's smile tightened, but he pressed on, unflinching. "That profit gave us the capital necessary to acquire state-owned enterprises during Yeltsin's privatization auctions in 1992. We paid mere pennies for massive assets—all under the carefully crafted guise of reinvestment promises."

Rybkin let out a deep, almost cruel laugh, his voice thick with irony. "Promises not worth the paper they were printed on! Admit it, Boris—we weren't chasing operational success. We wanted the assets, pure and simple. And we got them. Sure, we reinvested here and there—but only token amounts. Just enough to keep things running, while the real value slipped right into our hands."

The two men exchanged a glance, the weight of their shared history settling between them like smoke in a closed room— a story of ruthless ambition, sharp opportunism, and the merciless reshaping of a nation's fabric.

Boris shifted slightly in his seat, a subtle movement that did not escape Viktor's keen observation. Though it was almost imperceptible, Viktor sensed the undercurrent of discomfort beneath his employer's composed exterior. Despite being physically close to Boris during these business dealings, Viktor knew all too well that he was kept deliberately at arm's length from the oligarch's inner workings. The boundary between employer and employee was rigid and clear—one Boris had no intention of blurring. Yet beneath that polished veneer, Viktor couldn't shake the persistent feeling that Boris was uneasy, perhaps even guarded, about Rybkin's blunt candor.

"Careful, Vladimir," Boris cautioned quietly, his voice low but firm, carrying the weight of unspoken warnings. "We've made investments where it truly matters."

Rybkin, however, was undeterred. He waved his cigar with a dismissive flick, his tone sharp and unapologetic. "Small investments, Boris. Let's not pretend otherwise. That's precisely why the media has us under such intense scrutiny. Criticism is inevitable in our line of work. But what can anyone really do now? Not even the president himself can stop us from extracting the last fragments of value from these enterprises."

Rybkin's laughter echoed again in the confined space, rich and unrepentant, but it was abruptly cut off. With a soft, mechanical hum, the soundproof glass divider slid smoothly into place between the driver's cabin and the luxurious compartment behind, severing Viktor—and the chauffeur—from the conversation so effortlessly. The gesture was as deliberate as it was final, a subtle yet unmistakable reminder that certain truths were far too dangerous to be shared, even with the most trusted members of their staff.

Left alone in the quiet isolation of the limousine's front seat, Viktor stared straight ahead, the scattered city lights casting fractured patterns on his tense expression. He felt a strange blend of relief and unease settling deep in his chest. Whatever secrets lay just beyond that thin barrier had been consciously kept from him—and, in truth, he was certain they were better left unheard.

His gaze drifted past the passing buildings, their cold, imposing facades looming like silent sentinels guarding a world he could barely comprehend. The fragments of the conversation he had overheard echoed repeatedly in his mind, each word a sharp, inescapable reminder of just how distant his own reality was from the glittering, ruthless world inhabited by Boris Jumashyev—and the powerful men who shaped it.

Boris's rise to power was far more than just a success story—it was the kind of tale that tabloid journalists devoured eagerly, embellishing it as a rags-to-riches legend steeped in brilliance and ambition. Born into unassuming, humble beginnings, Boris had been a prodigy from an early age, dazzling his teachers with an innate aptitude for mathematics that seemed almost otherworldly. "A genius," proclaimed some papers, and Viktor had no reason to doubt it. For Boris, engineering wasn't simply a career choice—it was a destiny inherited from his father, a legacy of precision, intellect, and drive. Graduating at the very top of his class, Boris secured a coveted position at the Soviet Academy of Sciences within a year—a remarkable feat that marked the first step on an extraordinary climb. From that point, the ladder stretched ever upward, bolstered by well-cultivated Communist Party connections, until he ultimately became the director of the very fertilizer factory where Viktor's own father had labored away his entire life.

For Viktor, however, that factory symbolized a far darker reality. It was a place where hope had withered long ago; where men were ground down, reduced to nothing more than interchangeable cogs in an unforgiving, relentless machine. The chaotic days of 1992 played over and over in his mind, vivid and raw, as if they had happened only yesterday. He could still recall the electric tension in the air when Yeltsin's privatization program was announced—how adults whispered in anxious circles, grappling with uncertainty. His father had come home one evening clutching a government-issued ownership certificate, a voucher nominally worth ten thousand rubles. But instead of pride or hope, his father was wasted—drunk and too far gone to recognize its true significance.

[Historical note: In 1992, as part of Yeltsin's sweeping reforms, every Russian citizen was issued a voucher nominally worth 10,000 rubles, intended to give them a stake in the country's newly privatized enterprises. In practice, most people sold these vouchers for a fraction of their value, often to intermediaries or the emerging class of oligarchs.]

That night remained etched deeply in Viktor's memory. His father had staggered into their cramped apartment, slamming the certificate onto the kitchen table with the careless force of something worthless, like trash. At the time, Viktor hadn't understood the significance of his father's actions—the frustration, the resignation hidden beneath that drunken fury. Later, he learned the bitter truth: his father, like countless others, had sold his share at the local auction for next to nothing—right into the hands of men who understood its value far better.

The bitterness twisted inside Viktor now, as fiercely as it had back then. Those shares had represented so much more than paper or currency—they were symbols of opportunity, ownership, and a sliver of control over one's own destiny. But the workers hadn't known the vultures circling above, the men with sharp minds and sharper ambitions hovering to pick the carcass clean. Men like Boris, who swooped in and bought up those shares for a pittance, ascending swiftly to untouchable heights of wealth and power. Meanwhile, laborers like Viktor's father were left to scrape by, swallowed by a system designed to leave them behind.

Viktor's fists clenched tightly as the limousine glided smoothly through Moscow's grand avenues. Outside, the city flaunted its wealth unabashedly—stately architecture soaring upward, glittering lights illuminating every corner—but Viktor felt the fractures beneath the shine. Boris had treated his father's generation with cold indifference, and now he treated Viktor with the same chilling detachment. To

Boris, Viktor wasn't a man with hopes and struggles—he was simply another tool to be used and discarded when no longer convenient.

Yet beneath the simmering resentment in Viktor's chest, a flicker of defiance burned quietly but fiercely. He was not the helpless boy who had watched his father squander an opportunity. He was not the crushed man broken by an unforgiving system. He was here—seated in this sleek car, orbiting power and influence. And if there was one lesson Boris's story had taught him, it was this: the world never rewarded the meek. It belonged to those bold enough to seize it, to claim it by force if necessary. Viktor vowed silently that he would be one of those men.

Chapter 12

Viktor's gaze drifted over the towering facades of Moscow as the limousine glided smoothly through the winding city streets, each towering building seemed to hold its breath, steeped in silent stories of power, ruthless ambition, and relentless survival. The facades—ancient and modern alike—stood like silent witnesses to countless dramas played out behind their walls. Yet Viktor's mind remained firmly tethered to the weight of the conversation he had overheard earlier. The ambition, the cunning manipulation—it was a world he could only glimpse from the edges, a world that, despite its dazzling allure, left him deeply unsettled. Boris Jumashyev's rise was far more than a simple success story; it was a complex narrative soaked in contradictions. Born into modest beginnings, Boris had been a prodigy, a child celebrated for his uncanny brilliance with numbers and logic. The newspapers had called him a genius, and Viktor had no reason to doubt it.

As the limousine came to a smooth stop near the Kremlin, Viktor climbed out of the front seat and lifted his eyes to the towering Spasskaya Tower. Its ruby-red star caught the sunlight, shining like a beacon from a distant era, a symbol both timeless and imposing. The grandeur of the Kremlin was undeniable—majestic and overwhelming—but Viktor couldn't shake the persistent feeling that he was stepping onto a stage designed for someone else's story. The smooth marble beneath his feet and the polished opulence of the Kremlin's interiors were not meant for people like him—men pulled from humble origins, now thrust into the glittering orbit of power.

Yet, despite the dissonance, here he was.

Inside the Senate Building, Boris strode ahead with the kind of unshakable confidence that commanded attention and turned heads without effort. Viktor fell into step behind, taking his appointed place in the shadowed corner of the president's office. He stood straight, eyes sharp and observant, scanning every detail of the room—the heavy drapes, the ornate furniture, the subtle tension in the air. The atmosphere was thick with ambition's pulse—the kind that made men's voices rise and fall like well-rehearsed crescendos in a grand symphony of power.

Through the din, Viktor caught snippets of the president's grand vision—an ambitious Kremlin Center project intended to cement a lasting legacy. The scale was staggering, a bold endeavor projected to cost billions. "Luxury hotels, diamonds, opulence…" Boris's voice carried a tone of unmistakable approval, the glint in his eyes betraying a keen interest in the potential spoils.

Viktor's stomach churned as he absorbed the weight of it all. These were decisions that would shape the future of the nation itself—but they were made by men who moved enormous sums of money like chess pieces, indifferent to the countless lives beneath their gaze. Blending into the shadows, Viktor remained silent and invisible in the corner—a quiet observer, a shadow listening to the relentless machinations of power.

Hours later, Viktor found himself walking slowly across the vast expanse of Red Square, the fading evening sun casting long, stretched shadows over the ancient cobblestones beneath his feet. The vibrant energy of the square buzzed all around him—tourists clustered in animated groups, snapping photos and marveling at the iconic sights, their voices mingling in a lively chorus. Yet Viktor's mind was far from the joyful spectacle. A somber weight pressed deep within his chest, contrasting sharply with the lighthearted bustle surrounding him.

He had originally planned to visit one of Moscow's renowned museums, to immerse himself in art and history, hoping it might offer some comfort or distraction. But now the thought seemed distant and unattainable, overshadowed by doubts and the gnawing sense of displacement. Instead, he found his steps leading him toward GUM, the grand department store that had become a shining symbol of Russia's transformation—an emblem of the new wealth and conflicting realities defining this turbulent city.

As Viktor stepped inside the ornately designed GUM, the contrast struck him immediately. The soaring arches, delicate ironwork, and glass-paneled roofs made the space feel like stepping into an entirely different world. Crystal chandeliers cast a warm, golden light that shimmered off polished marble floors, and the faint scent of expensive perfume and polished wood filled the air. Elegant women floated past him, their heels clicking decisively on the floor like a rhythmic metronome marking a tempo he could neither follow nor escape. Their finely tailored coats, designer handbags, and sharp, assured gazes spoke of a world that Viktor could only observe from behind an invisible barrier. Every detail around him shimmered with unattainable luxury—the gilded storefronts with their glittering displays, the crisp suits displayed behind glass, the muted rustle of silk dresses as refined customers brushed past.

For a moment, Viktor's eyes caught his reflection in one of the glass display cases. He saw himself as if from a distance—a man caught straddling two worlds, belonging fully to neither. There was a subtle yearning lodged in his chest—not for wealth or glamour, but for a sense of control, a firm foothold in the ever-shifting and often ruthless landscape around him. Moscow had shown Viktor its dazzling splendor, yes, but it had also revealed its unforgiving cruelty. If there was one lesson he had learned on these streets, it was this: in a city like this, standing still was the same as falling behind. The world was harsh and relentless, and it rewarded only those with the courage to move forward, decisively and without hesitation.

Stepping back outside into the cool evening air, the chill brushing against his face like a reminder of reality, Viktor's resolve hardened. He might still find himself on the edges of this powerful world, but he refused to stay there forever. He would not become like his father, a man forced to watch opportunities slip silently through trembling fingers. If Moscow demanded ambition and decisiveness, Viktor would rise to meet it. He would forge his own path, claim his own stake.

With that newfound determination, Viktor set his course for one of the city's upscale men's boutiques. His steps were measured, his expression calm but charged with quiet determination. The boutique's sleek, polished interiors awaited him, and almost immediately, an impeccably dressed attendant appeared, their practiced smile as flawless as the elegant surroundings.

"A suit," Viktor said simply, his voice steady, carrying the weight of his resolve.

Within moments, an array of suits—tailored precisely to his measurements—was laid out before Viktor. Each piece bore prestigious labels and price tags that, not long ago, would have seemed nothing more than a distant, unattainable dream. A flicker of triumph ignited within him, a rare indulgence in this new world he was tentatively stepping into. The boutique's luxurious atmosphere enveloped him as he tried on one suit after another, savoring the feel of the fine fabrics against his skin. Each garment seemed to shed a layer of his old life, replacing it with something sharper, more refined, and more in tune with the persona he was beginning to craft.

Taking his time to assess every detail, Viktor finally settled on a dark blue Armani suit. Its deep hue complemented the crisp, folded shirts he paired with it—the kind of precise, immaculate presentation that spoke volumes without uttering a word.

With the bag in hand and the old clothes stuffed inside, Viktor felt a subtle surge of confidence as he stepped out of the boutique and made his way toward Kitay-Gorod. As he entered this historic district—a labyrinth of narrow, winding streets and weathered stone facades, once the bustling heart of Moscow's merchant class—the contrast struck him like a cold wind. The dense, aging buildings pressed close together, their peeling paint and faded grandeur a sharp counterpoint to the glittering boutiques and sleek modernity he had just left behind. The energy here was heavy, almost claustrophobic; what others might romanticize as quaint or charming felt to Viktor like an oppressive weight dragging him down. It was a gritty, less glamorous Moscow—a reminder that beneath the city's gleaming surface lay layers of history marked by struggle and hardship. Without hesitation, he decided this was not the place for him. He caught the next bus, letting its route carry him steadily northward toward the towering Ostankino TV Tower.

The massive structure loomed ahead, its spire piercing the sky at over 300 meters—a testament to Soviet engineering and ambition. Viktor stepped into the elevator and ascended swiftly to the observation deck. From this elevated vantage point, the sprawling panorama of Moscow unfurled before him—a mesmerizing, pulsating maze of life, movement, and endless possibility. The city's veins of streets and arteries of wide avenues pulsed with vitality, weaving a complex web of humanity beneath him. Amidst the vastness, Viktor felt both minuscule and invigorated, awed by the sheer scale and dynamism of it all.

The moment was shattered suddenly by a deep rumble in his stomach. Checking his watch, Viktor realized it had been nearly ten hours since breakfast. Hunger gnawed at him insistently, demanding immediate attention and pulling him back from his reverie to the practical realities of the day.

He chose the nearest restaurant he could find, grateful for a moment's respite from the day's relentless pace. Securing a seat by the window, Viktor positioned himself to continue admiring the sweeping cityscape beyond the glass. The lights of the sprawling metropolis twinkled faintly, creating a calm backdrop that contrasted with the turmoil in his mind.

When the server approached, Viktor kept his order simple but satisfying: a medium-rare steak and a pint of beer. The promise of a hearty meal was a small comfort after the long day.

Behind him, a boisterous group of overweight tourists filled the space with loud laughter and the incessant clinking of glasses. Their exuberance grated sharply against the restaurant's otherwise calm, muted ambiance, breaking the cozy quiet with a cacophony of careless joy. Yet Viktor, drawn inward, tuned them out effortlessly, focusing instead on the glittering city beyond the window.

When the steak arrived, any anticipation Viktor had felt curdled quickly into disappointment. The meat lay before him, nearly raw, bleeding heavily as his knife sliced through with little resistance. Each bite was tough, and a metallic tang lingered unpleasantly on his tongue—a far cry from the meal he had hoped for. Meanwhile, the waiter was nowhere to be found, preoccupied with cleaning up after a child's spilled drink at a nearby table. Complaining felt futile in that moment. Resigned, Viktor forced down several reluctant, unsatisfying bites before finally giving up and turning his attention to the beer. At least it tasted as it should—cold and crisp, its sharp bitterness offering a fleeting balm against the meal's shortcomings.

After the underwhelming meal, Viktor rose and made his way toward Tverskaya Street, one of Moscow's most renowned avenues. The street stretched out in front of him like a shimmering ribbon, lined on either side with glittering boutiques and opulent storefronts. Each window display was a carefully curated exhibit of wealth, luxury, and excess—designer goods gleaming unapologetically, their sky-high price tags a stark reminder of the elite world that pulsed at Moscow's heart.

At the far end of the avenue stood Piramida Bar, the epitome of exclusivity and prestige—a sleek, modern sanctuary for the city's nouveau riche. Viktor watched as a glamorous couple, effortlessly radiating confidence and privilege in every step, approached the entrance. Sensing an opportunity, he adjusted his posture and trailed closely behind them, hoping to blend in seamlessly with the fashionable crowd. It was a calculated risk, but one he felt compelled to take—a small step toward making this complex, dazzling city feel a little more like home.

But the ruse didn't work. Just inside the entrance, a burly doorman emerged from the shadows, his imposing frame blocking Viktor's path. The man's sharp, appraising gaze swept over Viktor's carefully chosen attire—the tailored Armani suit, the neat crease of his trousers, the subtle but confident way he carried himself. Yet none of it seemed to matter. With a quiet finality, the doorman shook his head.

"Sorry, it's full," he said, his tone indifferent and clipped, offering no room for argument.

Viktor's eyes flicked past the man, darting toward the lounge beyond where, to his disbelief, the space was clearly only half-occupied. Plush leather chairs scattered in small clusters, a few patrons lounging casually, laughter and music spilling softly into the air. The lie was obvious, yet the doorman remained unmoved, his expression unreadable.

Before Viktor could protest, the doorman grasped him firmly by the collar and pushed him forcefully back onto the street. Viktor stumbled, barely catching his balance. The physical shove stung less than the blow to his pride, sharp and biting. Straightening his suit jacket, he muttered under his breath, the words raw with frustration.

"Damn it," he snarled, casting a resentful glare at the bar's glowing neon sign that buzzed mockingly in the evening.

Turning away, Viktor began trudging back toward his hotel, the buoyant confidence he'd carried earlier in the day now replaced by a gnawing sense of rejection and invisibility. The surrounding streets blurred into a swirling haze, the city's dazzling lights reduced to distant echoes as his mind replayed the encounter over and over, the sting of dismissal echoing in every heartbeat.

As he rounded a familiar corner near Red Square, his phone vibrated sharply in his pocket, jolting him from his spiraling thoughts. He stopped abruptly, pulling the device from his jacket with shaking hands. The name flashing on the screen froze him in place.

Vladimir.

The very name was like a cold hand gripping his heart, dredging up memories he had tried to bury deep beneath layers of resolve. Vladimir—the childhood friend who had dragged him unwittingly into a world of violence and murder. A shadow that had never fully lifted.

His thumb hovered uncertainly over the decline button, every instinct screaming to ignore it. Yet, something deeper—an unspoken obligation or a flicker of unresolved loyalty—compelled him to answer.

"Hello," Viktor said, his voice tight, controlled—but trembling just beneath the surface, carrying the weight of old ghosts and the uneasy future they still threatened to shape.

"Viktor," Vladimir's voice came through the phone as casual and unbothered as if they were merely discussing the weather. There was an unsettling nonchalance underpinning his tone that immediately set Viktor on edge.

"Yeah, it's me," Viktor replied, swallowing hard against the sudden tightness in his throat. The image of the journalist's lifeless eyes flashed unbidden in his mind—vivid and haunting, etched into his memory as sharply as the day it had happened. No matter how much he tried to suppress it, the memory clung to him like a dark shadow, tainting every corner of his thoughts.

"I've got another job for you," Vladimir continued smoothly. "Pays well. Interested?"

Viktor's stomach twisted uneasily at the casual manner in which Vladimir spoke, as if the past had never happened. "No," he snapped, his voice taut with resolve and finality. "I'm done with that life. Done."

An oppressive silence followed—a heavy, charged pause that hung between them like a physical weight.

"I don't think you understand," Vladimir said, his voice dropping into something colder, sharper—laden with menace and danger. "Remember the knife?"

Viktor's breath caught sharply. The knife. The very weapon Vladimir had taken from him that fateful night.

"You didn't get rid of it?" Viktor's voice barely rose above a whisper, trembling with a mixture of dread and disbelief.

"No. Thought it might come in handy," Vladimir replied smoothly, the threat implicit in those words striking Viktor like a brutal blow to the stomach.

The knife, with Viktor's fingerprints smeared across it, was leverage—a noose tightening inexorably around his neck, a silent reminder of secrets best left buried.

Viktor's pulse hammered wildly, his breath quickening as panic and dread seeped slowly through his veins. The silence stretched taut once more before Vladimir broke it again, his tone calm but coiled tightly with quiet menace.

"So, you want to hear what I have in mind?"

Viktor closed his eyes, the last of his resistance crumbling under the immense weight of that unspoken threat. There was no escaping it—not without terrible cost.

"Fine," he muttered softly, his voice barely audible, strained and defeated. "What do you want?"

Chapter 13

A week later, the time had come to execute the mission. Viktor pulled the knit cap tightly down over his head, carefully tucking in every stray strand of hair to ensure nothing betrayed his presence. The snug fabric pressed firmly against his scalp, a constant, tangible reminder of the night's weighty purpose and the tension coursing through his veins. Dark streaks of camouflage paint streaked across his face, cold and slick against his skin, transforming him into a living shadow among shadows—a ghost moving unseen through the city's underbelly.

Around him, the city's muted hum pulsed softly, distant and indifferent to his mission. He crept silently along the damp, graffiti-stained wall of the aging tenement building, the cracked pavement muffling the whisper of his footsteps. At the corner, he stopped short and crouched low, pressing his back against the cold, worn stone. Leaning forward just enough to peer cautiously into the dimly lit backyard, he took in the sorry scene: a portrait of neglect and abandonment.

Overflowing trash cans lay in disarray, their refuse spilling out onto the ground like gaping open wounds. Shattered furniture and jagged scraps of rusted metal littered the space, faintly glinting beneath the pale, watchful gaze of the moon. A dilapidated delivery van sagged against the house wall, its battered body streaked with years of dirt and neglect; the tires had sunk deep into the cracked earth beneath. Once-bright paint had long since faded to a mottled, lifeless brown, peeling away like the memories this place had tried to bury.

Viktor narrowed his eyes, flicking his gaze toward the villa nestled at the center of the yard. The small wooden structure, with its peeling paint, warped planks, and sagging roofline, seemed hopelessly out of place—an aging relic trapped between the looming tenement and the skeletal steel framework of a nearby construction site. The half-built shopping center rose ominously into the sky like a cold promise of modernity, its scaffolding casting jagged, angular shadows that sliced across the villa's weary facade.

The villa's windows were dark and lifeless, blank eyes staring into the night.

Vladimir's words echoed in Viktor's ears with steady reassurance: "No one lives there anymore." He clung fiercely to those words, repeating them silently like a mantra, struggling to quell the storm of doubt gnawing at the edges of his mind.

The sharp air bit at his cheeks, with a coldness that nipped at the exposed skin of his fingers. He exhaled slowly, grateful that the air wasn't cold enough to betray him with clouds of vapor—each breath a potential signal to unseen watchers. The night felt oppressive and watchful, every faint rustle, every distant clatter amplified sharply by his heightened senses, as if the shadows themselves were holding their breath.

Without hesitation and with practiced ease, Viktor melted into the darkness and moved forward.

He darted suddenly from his hiding place, his movements sharp, precise, and controlled, as though every step carried the weight of his determination. His boots skimmed barely above the cracked pavement, making almost no sound as he closed the distance to the villa. The bottle of gasoline clenched tightly in his hand sloshed ominously with each step, its viscous weight a constant, tangible reminder of the task ahead—an act that would alter everything.

Reaching the side of the villa, Viktor dropped low instinctively, letting the heavy shadow cast by the building swallow him whole. The sharp, acrid tang of gasoline filled the cool night air as he unscrewed the cap of the bottle. He poured the thick liquid freely, watching it glisten and shine in the moonlight as it soaked into the dry, weathered wood, seeping into every crack and crevice of the old structure.

Viktor worked quickly but with meticulous care, ears pricked to catch any abnormal sound beyond the rhythmic splatter of the fuel hitting the surface. His hands trembled ever so slightly—an involuntary reaction to the raw, visceral nature of the act pressing down upon him like a suffocating weight. With steady resolve, he uncapped the second bottle and repeated the process, the final few drops soaking greedily into the parched timbers.

When the last precious drop of gasoline was spent, he straightened slowly, wiping his damp palms on his jacket, trying to quell the rapid beating of his heart. The air was thick with anticipation. Then, from a small inner pocket, he drew a matchbook, the thin cardboard feeling fragile and insignificant in his hands, yet containing the terrifying power to unleash complete devastation.

With a practiced flick of his thumb, a match ignited, its tiny flame dancing unsteadily in the stillness—a fragile beacon amidst the darkness. Viktor's breath caught, his chest tightening as he hurled the fiery spark toward the fuel-soaked house.

The gasoline erupted with a sharp hiss, flames leaping to life like a ravenous beast awakened. The fire clawed hungrily along the villa's weathered walls, spreading upward with terrifying speed as tongues of orange and red licked the night sky. Within seconds, the entire structure was bathed in a roaring glow, waves of heat radiating outward, prickling Viktor's skin even from a distance.

He moved swiftly away, retreating to the relative safety of the tenement's shadowed corner. From the darkness, he watched with wide, unblinking eyes as the fire devoured its target. The brittle, ancient wood crackled and groaned, every snap, pop, and creak sounding like a scream caught in the belly of the night. Acrid smoke coiled and twisted upward, its sharp, choking stench filling Viktor's lungs with each breath. The flames leapt higher and higher, their furious glow reflected in the stark lines of his tense face.

His fingers dug deep into the cold, rough surface of the brick wall, steadying his trembling body as he fought to regulate his ragged breathing. The villa's walls began to buckle and collapse inward, the sound reverberating through the sleeping neighborhood like a thunderous exclamation point punctuating the moment's finality. Viktor's pulse raced, pounding against his ribs as the weight of what had transpired crashed fully upon him.

It's empty, he told himself again, the mantra hollow and fragile against the roar of the inferno. No one is inside.

But despite the repetition, despite the desperate quiet of those words, Viktor couldn't silence the gnawing doubt clawing relentlessly at the edges of his mind—an uneasy whisper that refused to let him rest.

Chapter 14

Viktor stared out the airplane window at the vast, shimmering expanse of the azure sea below, where palm trees swayed gently in the warm breeze. The scene was picturesque and almost dreamlike—a sharp contrast to the turmoil churning inside him. The French Riviera, with its sun-drenched coastline and glittering waters, was a place he had long fantasized about visiting, imagining excitement and escape. Yet now, as the plane began its slow descent toward the runway, the thrill he once expected was conspicuously absent. Instead, a heavy, oppressive weight clung to him like an unshakable shadow, dragging him deeper into the dark recesses of his thoughts.

The fire haunted him relentlessly.

Why had someone hired him to torch that decrepit, forgotten villa? Who were these faceless players lurking behind the scenes, and what exactly were they pursuing through such ruthless means? Vladimir's half-spoken hints echoed in Viktor's mind, fragments of a puzzle that seemed deliberately obscured. With limited information, Viktor could only speculate—but the answers likely lay buried deep within the tangled complexities of Russia's property laws.

Before 1991, private land ownership didn't exist in Russia—even owning the ground beneath a building was forbidden. That rigid system began to unravel with the introduction of the Land Code of 2001, legislation that finally granted building owners the right to claim ownership of the land beneath their structures. But there was a crucial stipulation: if a building ceased to exist, the owner forfeited the right to purchase that land altogether. The decaying walls Viktor had set ablaze days ago had stood as the final barrier blocking someone's ambitious plan for acquisition and redevelopment.

Lost in thought, Viktor barely noticed as the plane's wheels met the tarmac with a jarring thud, the sudden impact wrenching him back from his reverie. His grip tightened on the armrest as the seatbelt cinched snugly across his midsection and the aircraft began to decelerate sharply. His stomach churned with a mixture of anticipation and unease. The land in question was clearly valuable—prime real estate in the heart of Moscow, a location coveted by many and worth untold sums.

His eyes shifted toward Boris, seated calmly a few rows away. The question that gnawed at him, relentless and unresolved, remained: who had paid him to do this? And more perplexing still—why hadn't those powerful people simply done it themselves? The thought spun through his mind, a tangled knot of suspicion and doubt that refused to loosen. He couldn't help but wonder—did Boris know more than he let on? Was the oligarch somehow connected to the tangled web of questions that haunted his mind?

The heat struck Viktor like an overwhelming wave as he stepped off the plane, wrapping around him in a sweltering, suffocating embrace. Within moments, beads of sweat began to trickle down his back, soaking into the fabric of his shirt and clinging to his skin. The air felt thick and heavy, laden not only with heat but with the invisible weight of unresolved doubts and unanswered questions pressing relentlessly on his thoughts. He hurried toward the waiting limousine, relieved to find sanctuary in its cool, air-conditioned interior. Sinking into the soft leather seat, he gazed out the window at the city rushing past, his mind spinning in an endless, restless loop.

Beside him, Boris sat completely at ease, his posture relaxed as he engaged in a phone call that quickly drew Viktor's attention. The unmistakable tone of someone accustomed to power and control echoed from Boris's voice—it was sharp, commanding, and resolute.

"Listen," Boris said, his voice clipped and direct, "if you want results, you'll have to move faster." He reclined slightly in the plush seat, pausing to nod as if the person on the other end of the line could see his gestures.

"No delays," he continued firmly. "The investors won't wait forever."

Viktor's ears perked up. The tone in Boris's voice had shifted, becoming sharper, tinged with impatience and the unmistakable pressure of high stakes.

"I don't care how complicated the permits are," Boris snapped, his voice laced with authority. "That's your job."

A long silence stretched as Boris listened intently, his fingers drumming lightly and rhythmically against the armrest. The weight of the conversation settled heavily in the confined space, and Viktor strained to piece together its meaning, a creeping unease tightening around his chest like a vice.

"Yes, that plot," Boris said at last, his tone measured but firm, unmistakably resolute. "The one adjacent to the shopping center."

Viktor stiffened instantly, his heart picking up pace. His eyes darted toward Boris, who now cast a casual, almost indifferent gaze out the window, betraying nothing. Yet for Viktor, the mention of that parcel of land was a jarring reminder—a stark connection to the fire, the villa, and the deeper forces at play beyond his understanding.

"Well, it's been handled," Boris continued with a casual nonchalance that belied the gravity of his words. "The details are irrelevant. Just make sure the acquisition is finalized. No mistakes."

He ended the call with a deliberate press of a button, his lips curling into a faint, satisfied smile that spoke volumes. Viktor's heart pounded in his chest, adrenaline spiking suddenly. Had he just heard confirmation? Was Boris, in fact, behind the fire that had consumed the villa? The implication sent a cold shiver through him, raising more questions than answers.

The limousine snaked through the serene French countryside as the hustle and glare of the city gave way to rolling vineyards and rustic charm. Verdant rows of grapevines stretched endlessly toward the horizon, their orderly patterns a striking contrast to the tangled webs Viktor was caught in back in Moscow. When they finally arrived at the château, Viktor stepped out of the vehicle, blinking against the harsh, bright sunlight. The estate was breathtaking in its grandeur: ancient oaks cast long, cool shadows over immaculately kept grounds, and a stately moat encircled the château itself, its glassy surface reflecting the pale blue sky above like a still mirror.

[135]

Yet Viktor barely registered the beauty surrounding him. His thoughts clung stubbornly to Boris's phone call, the terse words echoing in his mind like an unresolved riddle he could neither decipher nor escape.

Boris stepped out beside him, already pulling his phone from his pocket to answer another call. His demeanor remained perfectly composed—every movement purposeful and calm, as if the weight of their conversations was no heavier than a casual stroll through the countryside. For Viktor, however, a storm of doubt and guilt brewed silently beneath this tranquil façade, threatening to break at any moment.

Two elegant English setters bounded energetically across the manicured lawn, their sleek, muscular bodies slicing through the warm afternoon air. Behind them strolled a man in his early sixties, gray-haired but vigorous, dressed casually in jeans and a crisp white T-shirt. A cigarette dangled lazily between his fingers, wisps of smoke curling upward in slow, graceful spirals. His broad grin spread widely across his face, radiating an easy, casual confidence. Boris returned the smile, his own gesture expansive and inviting, clearly at ease.

The way Boris threw his arms open made it clear to Viktor that this casually dressed man was likely the owner of the estate.

"Jakov Kalinin," the gray-haired man announced warmly as he extended his hand to Boris.

The two men clasped hands firmly, their conversation immediately sparking to life with animated energy. Kalinin's hearty laughter mingled with Boris's measured, calm responses as the estate owner began leading him on a tour of the sprawling property. Viktor fell a few steps behind, his sharp eyes meticulously scanning the surroundings while his ears caught fragments of the exchange. Although Kalinin spoke Russian passably, his accent betrayed years spent abroad, adding another layer of intrigue to the encounter.

As they walked toward the stables, it quickly became clear that Jakov Kalinin was an American citizen of Russian descent. Suddenly, Kalinin stopped and pivoted to face Boris, his expression shifting into one of theatrical enthusiasm, as if eager to share a story he had long cherished.

"My fascination with French estates began during a trip to France in the eighties," Kalinin declared, his voice swelling with vibrant excitement. "I found a château I thought was absolutely breathtaking and bought it. But then, as fate would have it, I discovered another—far more beautiful. Naturally, I had to add that one to my collection. By the time I stumbled upon a third estate, well, how could I resist?" He spread his hands wide, as though the logic behind his acquisition spree was indisputable and self-evident.

Boris raised a skeptical eyebrow, clearly intrigued by this revelation. "Quite the collector, I see," he remarked, a hint of admiration mingling with curiosity in his tone.

Kalinin chuckled deeply, the sound warm and rich. "Ah, but it wasn't always smooth sailing," he admitted, lowering his voice to a confidential whisper, as though sharing a well-guarded secret. "When I bought my first estate, I was summoned to a town hall meeting. Imagine that! Can you believe it?"

[137]

"Oh? What was the issue?" Boris prompted, his tone polite yet genuinely curious.

Kalinin leaned in slightly, his voice dropping even lower. "The French, you see, don't take kindly to foreigners buying up their heritage. It's not common for an outsider to come here and pour money into centuries-old properties like this. And believe me, it's not exactly a lucrative endeavor, either." A sly twinkle danced in his eyes as he added with a mock-serious shrug, "Naturally, the locals couldn't understand that I simply loved the countryside. Rumors started flying— whispers that I was running some sort of cult!"

Boris laughed, the sound genuine and hearty. "And how did you handle that?" he asked, amused.

Kalinin grinned broadly, as though recalling the absurdity of the situation with fondness.

"Well, fortunately, I managed to convince the twenty skeptics at that town hall meeting that I wasn't some deranged cult leader," Kalinin said, his grin broadening with fond amusement. "I'm no actor, but I can spin a hell of a tale when I need to." His eyes twinkled as he recalled the moment. "Nowadays, the local authorities know me quite well. Why, when I hosted a car exhibition here on the estate, the mayor and the police chief both showed up. Naturally, I made sure there was plenty to eat and drink for everyone." He burst into a hearty laugh, the sound rolling across the grounds like a ripple of thunder. "The police chief," he wheezed between chuckles, "had such a good time that we pretty much had to carry him out—in full uniform, no less— along with a very inebriated mayor!"

Boris joined in the laughter, his amusement genuine as his eyes briefly drifted toward a large garage sitting across from the stables. His gaze lingered there, curiosity flickering in the depths of his expression.

Noticing Boris's interest, Kalinin's grin didn't falter. "Tell me," he said with a sly tone, "are you a car enthusiast?"

Boris nodded eagerly, the spark of curiosity shining openly in his eyes. "I can't deny it. I've heard you own quite a collection."

"That's correct," Kalinin replied, his chest puffing just a little with pride. He launched into a confident list as though cataloging precious treasures: "About twenty Ferraris, five Lamborghinis, an Aston Martin, a Bentley, a couple of Rolls-Royces, some Jaguars, and Mercedes-Benz models—just to name a few." He paused, his eyes gleaming with mischievous intent. "But you know," he added with a playful grin, "I've always wanted to add a Volga to the collection."

"I can probably arrange that," Boris said promptly, a flash of keen business acumen in his voice.

"Fantastic, I'd really appreciate it," Kalinin responded, clearly pleased by the offer. Then, with a chuckle, he added, "But honestly, I'm a terrible driver. As much as I'm crazy about cars, it's real horsepower that holds my heart."

"Oh, really?" Boris asked, smoothly steering the conversation away from Jakov's confessed lack of driving skills. "How many horses do you have?"

"Let me think…" Kalinin pondered for a moment, his voice bright with genuine enthusiasm. "I believe it's around 125 to

130 in total. I keep stables here on the estate, two more scattered across France, and one just outside London in England."

He turned to Boris with a broad, almost boyish smile. "I absolutely adore those animals! Working with horses gives me a much greener image than just being a car enthusiast. You see what I mean?"

Boris nodded with a knowing smile. "Absolutely. A green profile is all the rage these days."

"It certainly is," Kalinin agreed, the tone of his voice taking on an earnest edge. "But environmentalism isn't just a fashionable gimmick for me." He took a slow drag from his third cigarette since their arrival, the smoke curling lazily upward. "As I've grown older, I've become increasingly concerned about my health and preserving the nature we all depend on."

He paused for a moment, his eyes reflecting a rare vulnerability. "I've hardly been sick in my entire life. For the longest time, I wasn't even sure I could die. To me, it was always a question of if I'd die, not when. But now? Now I know with certainty that I'm going to die—and that it might happen sooner than I'd like. You understand…"

Kalinin's tone turned somber, the weight of the admission settling heavily between them.

"I was diagnosed with skin cancer a few years ago, which isn't surprising, really," he admitted with a wry smile. "I have very fair skin, the sun here is incredibly intense, and I've never used sunscreen. And I still don't—I absolutely can't stand the smell of perfume. The only cream I use is toothpaste," he added with a chuckle, patting Boris on the back in a friendly, almost conspiratorial way.

"That's why staying in shape has become so important to me," he continued, his grin broadening once again. "I don't box or jog or any of that stuff, but I find kissing girls is a lot of fun—and believe me, that's a sport in itself." His booming laughter rang out, his eyes sparkling with teasing mischief.

"I'm doing pretty damn well these days. Plenty of time, enough money, and…" Kalinin slung an arm casually over Boris's shoulder with the ease of an old friend. "You see… after selling off all my properties and businesses in the U.S., I was left with a nice pile of cash. Now, I do exactly what I feel like doing—namely, nothing but having fun. You know what I mean?"

Boris nodded in response, but Viktor could tell his boss didn't truly grasp how someone could find joy in spending time purely on pleasure and games. For Boris, success was measured in profits and power. While he had no objection to spending money, it was only when such spending served a clear purpose—whether advancing his business interests or consolidating influence. The idea of spending lavishly purely for enjoyment, or giving without expecting a return, was foreign to him. Viktor had never once seen Boris toss a coin to a beggar on the street. The oligarch was famously guarded, sharing little of himself beyond what was necessary. His interactions with employees like Viktor were strictly professional, marked by a cool distance and an absence of personal warmth. Even when Viktor received bonuses or occasional praise, such acknowledgments were

[141]

rare and felt perfunctory. Recognition simply wasn't a language Boris spoke fluently.

Kalinin's voice broke through Viktor's reflections. "You might've noticed the limp?" he said casually. "I wrecked my leg a couple of years ago. Haven't been able to ride as much as I'd like since then."

Viktor looked up, intrigued despite himself.

"I was out working the land here, trying to dislodge a rock that had jammed the bulldozer," Kalinin continued, shaking his head with a wry smile at the memory. "Next thing I know, I slammed my leg straight into the belt. Hurt like hell! Luckily, I didn't lose the damn thing."

The casualness of the confession struck Viktor. For all Kalinin's wealth and status, the man was startlingly rough around the edges—far removed from the polished image one might expect of a wealthy château owner. His graying hair jutted out in wild tufts, as though no comb had dared to approach it in some time. The plain white T-shirt he wore seemed to have long since surrendered its battle to remain tucked into his faded, worn jeans.

Viktor found himself both amused and bemused. Kalinin was a contradiction—a man with the means to lead a refined, polished life, yet possessing the temperament of someone completely indifferent to convention or appearances. The image clashed sharply with Viktor's preconceived notions, leaving him momentarily off balance and unsure how to reconcile the two.

"This has been all about me," Jakov Kalinin said with a sheepish grin, breaking the silence. "Why don't we turn the spotlight over to you? What kind of horse are you looking for? A riding horse, or a racehorse?"

"A racehorse," Boris replied without hesitation. "It's a gift for my daughter. She's studying political science in Moscow and has only a year left before she graduates." His voice carried unmistakable pride, the affection for his daughter softening the usual steel in his tone. The thought of bestowing such a prestigious gift hinted at layers of family expectations and hopes buried beneath his business facade.

"She's exceptionally bright and works incredibly hard," Boris said, his voice softening with a father's pride. "Her goal is to become an ambassador. I thought a racehorse would be the perfect gift—something prestigious, something that symbolizes both grace and determination. But it has to be well-trained. I want her to have a winner."

"Then I might have just the one for you," Jakov Kalinin replied, his eyes sparkling with genuine enthusiasm. Without waiting for a response, he hobbled off toward an aging van parked precariously on a slope near the stables. Its faded paint was chipped and peeling, and the dented body bore the scars of years of heavy use and relentless wear.

Kalinin clambered into the driver's seat, muttering to himself as he wrestled with the stubborn gearbox. A loud clank echoed in the quiet estate as the van groaned in protest, then lurched abruptly backward with unexpected, alarming speed. The tires spun wildly in the loose gravel, throwing up a thick cloud of dust that hung suspended in the warm afternoon air. With a resounding CRACK, the van slammed violently into the paddock fence, sending splinters and shards of wood flying in every direction, like confetti in a chaotic, uncontrolled celebration.

The two horses inside the paddock, who had been lazily swatting flies with their tails moments before, froze mid-swing. Their ears shot upright, and wide, startled eyes locked onto the van with a raw, primal fear. As if on cue, the animals bolted, galloping madly in tight circles, their hooves thundering against the earth in a frantic, panicked rhythm.

Kalinin peered through the rear window, a bemused expression flickering across his face—somewhere between sheepish amusement and mild annoyance at his own clumsiness. He slid out of the van, waving a dismissive hand at the broken fence. "Just a scratch!" he called nonchalantly, as though the shattered wood was nothing more than a minor inconvenience. "Come on, let's head to the stables!"

Boris and Viktor exchanged incredulous glances but, accustomed to Kalinin's rough charm, followed his lead without hesitation. They had barely stepped through the white stable doors when an ominous creak echoed from the slope behind them. They turned just in time to witness the van—the same aging, unpredictable vehicle—rolling toward them, gathering speed like an ungainly juggernaut on a collision course.

The gravity of the moment pressed down as they braced themselves for the inevitable chaos yet to unfold.

"Watch out!" Viktor shouted, his voice sharp and urgent as he leapt sideways with a sudden burst of energy, narrowly avoiding the lumbering van barreling toward them.

Kalinin sprang into action immediately, his legs pumping furiously as he gave chase to stop the runaway vehicle. One hand clutched tightly to his hat, struggling to keep it from flying off in the rush, while the other reached wildly for the driver's-side door handle. He grabbed it with a determined grip, but the loose gravel at his feet betrayed him, causing his shoes to skid and slide as he fought to plant his feet firmly. The van, seemingly unfazed by his efforts, dragged him along like a reluctant dance partner unwilling to follow the rhythm.

"Whoa! Stop, you stubborn old mule!" Kalinin shouted, his voice a strange mix of amusement and panic, the words tumbling out as he half-laughed, half-yelled in frustration.

Finally, with a loud, grinding thud, the van came to an abrupt halt, crashing gently yet decisively against the imposing stable doors. Kalinin, now thoroughly out of breath but grinning with the adventurous spirit of a man who had just narrowly escaped disaster, climbed free and dusted off his hands with a theatrical flourish. He turned to Boris and Viktor, gesturing toward the stable in a grand, unbothered manner.

"Well, there we are," he said as though nothing unusual had taken place, his tone light and conspiratorial. "Let's take a look at those horses, shall we?"

Boris managed to stifle a laugh behind his hand, the absurdity of the situation momentarily breaking his usual composure. Viktor, however, couldn't help but let out a genuine chuckle, shaking his head in disbelief at the chaotic charm of Kalinin's antics.

The moment underscored the unpredictable, unpolished character of the estate's owner—a man who lived life with a reckless humor that was as captivating as it was confounding.

Chapter 15

Summer 2006

The Queen Anne Stakes were just moments away, marking the grand commencement of the Royal Ascot races—a storied tradition that stretched back nearly two centuries. Since 1840, the event had celebrated the legacy of the monarch who had founded Ascot Racecourse in 1711, blending centuries of heritage with the glamorous spectacle of high society. The heat shimmered over the throng gathered below, an invisible veil rippling above a sea of eager anticipation and whispered excitement. Laughter and low murmurings wove through the open stands, punctuated occasionally by the sharp, celebratory pop of champagne corks escaping their bottles.

Viktor, now a seasoned bodyguard after nearly a year in Boris's employ, stood discreetly in the corner of the private box that his employer had rented for the day. His stance was purposeful yet unobtrusive—alert without being obtrusive— as his sharp gaze flicked across the luxurious space, quietly taking in every detail of the scene. The guests were resplendent in their finest attire: men in tailored suits and crisp ties, women in elegant gowns and impossibly wide-brimmed hats that seemed to belong more on a runway than at a horse race. They nibbled delicately at trays of intricate hors d'oeuvres, their laughter mingling seamlessly with the low hum of the crowd and the distant thudding of hooves on turf below.

Each guest was a conspicuous embodiment of wealth, fame, or often, both. Viktor's eyes noted with a quiet, analytical

[147]

detachment how many faces bore the unmistakable imprint of a surgeon's hand—pursed lips stretched tight, cheeks lifted unnaturally, and eyes that somehow seemed less expressive beneath the tension of cosmetic alteration. To his left, a rail-thin American woman in her forties caught his attention briefly; her lips were unnaturally plumped to the point that they reminded Viktor, painfully, of Donald Duck's exaggerated beak.

At least there were a few natural beauties among the crowd, Viktor thought, his gaze drifting to a pair of young women nearby. Possibly twins, perhaps in their early twenties, they stood tall and slender, their flawless features untouched by artifice. Their sea-green eyes sparkled vividly against sun-kissed skin, and honey-blonde hair cascaded effortlessly over their bronzed shoulders, catching the light with a soft, golden sheen. They moved with the grace of dancers, their presence a reminder of youth and untouched elegance amid the carefully curated façades surrounding them.

As the excitement in the grandstands swelled and the horses prepared to thunder onto the track, Viktor remained vigilant, the world of opulence and spectacle juxtaposed sharply against the ever-present undercurrent of power, risk, and hidden agendas swirling just beneath the surface.

Across the room, Boris stood deep in animated conversation with Jakov Kalinin and a younger man Viktor didn't recognize, their voices blending into the soft murmur of the gathering. Nearby, Boris's daughter occupied a quieter space, her presence offering a subtle contrast to the dazzling glamour embodied by the twins Viktor had noticed earlier. Observing her from the corner of his eye, Viktor took in her understated charm—a different kind of allure that didn't scream for attention but quietly commanded it.

She was petite, barely reaching 165 centimeters, with a solid, compact frame that suggested strength and resilience rather than delicate fragility. Her round face was softened by high cheekbones, lending her an almost classical warmth. Dark, bold brows framed her deep brown eyes, which held a steady, thoughtful gaze. Her nose was broad but delicately shaped, leading down to full, expressive lips. Her chestnut-brown hair was pulled back with meticulous care into a sleek bun resting at the nape of her neck, emphasizing the gentle curve of her neck and shoulders. She wasn't conventionally beautiful by society's flashy standards, but there was something undeniably captivating about her—a quiet magnetism that set her apart.

As though sensing his gaze, she turned abruptly, her eyes locking onto his with an intensity that startled him. Viktor didn't have the luxury of looking away. Their eyes met—her brown ones steady and curious, his steel-gray ones unflinching and measured. To his surprise, a gentle, almost shy smile broke across her face, softening her features.

Viktor held her gaze, allowing his lips to curve into a faint smile in return. Her cheeks tinged with a delicate flush, the sudden vulnerability revealed in that moment catching him completely off guard. What was it about her that unsettled him so? He wondered as the strange feeling settled deep in his chest. Was it the softness within her eyes? The quiet sincerity in her smile? Or something more elusive, a subtle connection that whispered just beyond the edge of understanding.

A burst of light, feminine laughter shattered his reverie, yanking him firmly back to the present. He straightened, shaking away the unexpected distraction, and refocused on his duties with practiced precision, his eyes scanning the private box for any signs of trouble or need.

The men gathered in the room were immaculate in traditional morning suits—dark gray or black trousers sharply creased, paired with black jackets that fit like armor. Crisp white shirts peeped from beneath pale gray vests, and matching ties completed their ensemble with understated elegance. The women matched their partners' elegance, dressed in conservative yet striking ensembles, their outfits crowned by extravagant hats that ranged from delicately floral to boldly architectural.

Together, the guests embodied a world steeped in tradition and refinement, their polished appearances a carefully maintained veneer over the undercurrents of ambition and intrigue that permeated the day's grand proceedings.

A few feet away, a red-haired English lady caught Viktor's eye, her appearance made unforgettable not only by her vivid hair but by a pronounced overbite that gave her a peculiar charm. She wore a hat that resembled a sleeping cat curled delicately atop her head—a whimsical yet oddly fitting accessory that somehow encapsulated the eccentricity of the event. Nearby, a striking German woman—known to be married to a wealthy industrial magnate—precariously balanced what looked like a massive white "wedding cake" of a hat. Its layers towered upward, ornate and detailed, drawing admiring stares as well as covert glances of envy.

The German woman's voice suddenly rose above the general murmurs, cutting sharply through the warm hum of conversation as she recounted a recent incident with a sharp edge of indignation. "An English countess remarked that it's becoming a serious issue, with these nouveau riche barging into the royal enclosure," she declared, her tone a mixture of disbelief and disdain. A sharp, biting laugh escaped her lips as she shook her head dramatically. "And then, can you believe it? She had the audacity to glare at us as we walked past! Imagine such arrogance!"

Another guest, intrigued and amused, leaned in closer with a smirk playing on his lips. "What did you say to her?"

The German woman straightened with regal poise, her lips curling into a wry, knowing smile. "Oh, I simply said, 'If we're intruding, it must be because we have something you've lost: money.'" Her laughter rang out, confident and delighted by her own sharp wit, drawing approving chuckles from those nearby.

Having just completed his careful inspection of the private box, Viktor glanced back toward his boss. A subtle nod from Boris confirmed that everything was in order. With quiet satisfaction, Viktor retreated to his usual corner, where the shadows provided a welcome sense of detachment and invisibility. Over time, he had grown accustomed to the spectacle of extravagant and often absurd hats that defined the Ascot experience. But today, even he couldn't deny that Jelena looked particularly elegant. She wore a snow-white, knee-length dress that complemented her figure with tasteful simplicity, paired with a bold, signal-red pillbox hat that made a striking contrast. The vivid pop of red lent her an air

[151]

of understated confidence and unmistakable presence amidst the sea of flamboyance.

"I can't believe she's wearing red at Ascot," one of the women near Viktor muttered softly, half to herself, her voice tinged with a mix of surprise and disapproval.

"Why not?" another woman whispered back, her tone laced with quiet admiration. "It's bold. It suits her perfectly."

A ripple of excitement suddenly swept through the crowd, drawing everyone's attention toward the rail. At precisely 2:00 p.m., the unmistakable silhouette of Queen Elizabeth II's elegant carriage rolled gracefully onto the racetrack. A hush descended over the aristocratic spectators, their breath collectively held for a moment before they scrambled almost comically to raise their binoculars in unison, eager to catch every detail.

"Look, there's Prince Philip!" a voice whispered eagerly, tinged with reverence.

Another responded, "And there's the Earl of Wessex. Doesn't he look particularly dashing today?"

The presence of the royals was a fixture at these races—a living symbol of heritage, tradition, and exclusivity. Ever mindful of preserving that sense of aristocratic prestige, the Queen had recently established a new elite section called The Queen's Lawn, aiming to restore the grandeur of the royal tribune which had faced softened entry rules in recent years.

Jelena's horse, a gift from her father, was set to compete in one of the day's most anticipated races. Now that the Queen had arrived and the formalities were in place, the real spectacle could finally begin.

Jelena moved restlessly around the private box, her excitement as palpable as the tension in the air. Her fingers nervously toyed with the knot of hair at the nape of her neck, while her other hand traced soft, absent-minded circles along the stem of her champagne glass. Her eyes flitted anxiously toward the track below, reflecting a mixture of hope and nervous anticipation.

"I hope she wins," Jelena murmured, her voice barely audible, but Viktor caught every word. She glanced up at Boris, her tone edging upward with an urgency born of expectation. "She has to win. Right, Papa?"

Boris met her gaze with a confident, reassuring smile and placed a firm hand on her shoulder. "Of course she'll win. I wouldn't have bought her if I didn't believe in her. Trust me."

Jelena nodded, though her eyes betrayed a lingering uncertainty. "I just don't want her to disappoint," she admitted softly.

With a gentle chuckle, Boris responded, "Relax, my dear. She won't."

At exactly 2:30 p.m., the first race was called to start. Gleaming, muscular horses were led methodically into their starting gates, each jockey adorned in a kaleidoscope of colorful silks that fluttered like flags in the breeze. The gates clanged open with a sharp metallic bang, and the horses surged forward in a thunderous stampede, hooves pounding decisively against the lush turf.

Jelena and Boris leaned so far over the edge of the box that Viktor briefly feared they might topple. Their entire focus was consumed by the race unfolding below.

"Go, go!" Jelena shouted, her voice rising above the roaring din of the crowd. The usual decorum dissolved entirely as the spectators erupted into a chaotic symphony of shouts, cheers, and frantic gestures, all urging their chosen mounts to victory. The energy in the air was electric, a wild and exhilarating celebration of tradition, competition, and hope.

Viktor stepped out of the shadows, positioning himself Viktor stood directly behind Jelena, ostensibly watching the race, but his attention remained riveted on her. Despite the clamor and the flurry of activity around them, he couldn't shake the overwhelming urge to reach out, to bridge the invisible distance between them. When she suddenly took a small step backward, momentarily unsteady, Viktor's instincts kicked in. He reached out quickly, his hand closing gently around her arm to steady her as though she might fall.

"Careful," he murmured softly, his voice low and attentive, barely audible over the thunderous noise of the crowd.

Jelena turned toward him, her expression shy and startled, eyes wide as if caught off guard by his sudden touch. "Thank you," she whispered, her voice delicate and almost lost beneath the roar of the race.

When Viktor smiled at her, a faint, shy flush crept across her cheeks, painting them a delicate shade of pink. She quickly averted her gaze, an almost imperceptible flutter of vulnerability passing between them.

Meanwhile, the race intensified on the track below as the horses thundered toward the finish line. At the front, three fierce competitors vied for dominance, their jockeys crouched low in their saddles, urging their mounts with every fiber of will and skill. From the main pack, a sleek gray horse suddenly surged forward with astonishing speed, gaining ground inch by frantic inch on the black leader. The tension in the air was electric, almost palpable, as the finish line approached rapidly.

"Come on!" Boris roared, his voice raw and urgent, a Cuban cigar clenched firmly between his teeth, adding to the dramatic intensity of the moment.

The black and gray horses raced neck and neck, every powerful stride a blur of muscle and determination. Jelena bounced nervously on her heels, her excitement bubbling uncontrollably as she shouted words of encouragement with fervent passion.

"There! Go, go!" Her voice cracked with emotion as the horses crossed the finish line, the outcome hanging on a knife's edge.

For a suspended moment, it was impossible to tell who had won. The entire crowd collectively held its breath, eyes fixed intently on the judges. Then, a metallic voice crackled through the loudspeakers, announcing the victor. Jubilation swept like wildfire through the stands as Jelena's horse was declared the winner.

Her face lit up with unrestrained joy, radiant and triumphant. Without hesitation, she threw her arms around Boris, laughter bubbling freely from her lips as if all the tension and nerves of the day had dissipated in that single, victorious moment.

Jakov Kalinin, his face flushed with excitement and pride, clapped Boris firmly on the back. "I told you I sold you the best horse in the world!" he declared with a broad, triumphant grin.

Boris smiled back, a rare note of genuine warmth softening his usual guarded demeanor. "Best purchase I've ever made," he replied, his voice carrying an unusual note of satisfaction and pride.

Hugs and congratulations rippled through the private box as champagne corks popped one after another, sending tiny bursts of celebration into the air. The sparkling liquid flowed freely, glistening in elegant flutes and crystal glasses—a fitting tribute to the day's exhilarating success. The mood was electric, charged with triumph and release, as everyone savored the rare glow of victory in this exclusive enclave of high society.

The win naturally called for celebration, and Jelena, buoyed by excitement and youthful energy, along with her circle of wealthy young friends, spontaneously decided to continue the festivities in London. This sudden plan placed Viktor firmly in charge of watching over her, a responsibility he accepted with quiet determination.

Hours later, Viktor found himself standing in the midst of an exclusive nightclub, a temple of opulence and privilege. The dimly lit room was alive with a kaleidoscope of flashing lights that danced across polished surfaces, while throbbing music pulsed rhythmically through the dense air. Even the very atmosphere seemed thick with extravagance and indulgence, as though wealth had given substance to the air itself.

Among the eclectic crowd was the son of the English Crown Prince, recognizable by his confident demeanor and understated but expensive attire. His arm was casually draped around a strikingly dressed young woman who danced close to him, her movements bold and suggestive under the shimmering club lights. Viktor, rooted firmly in his role as quiet observer and protector, noted that neither the prince nor his companion appeared to acknowledge Jelena or her international circle of friends. Yet, this lack of recognition seemed to do nothing to diminish the exuberance of the Russian group, who threw themselves into dancing and drinking with a carefree abandon Viktor found both bewildering and foreign.

Jelena moved gracefully across the dance floor, her champagne glass catching and fracturing the multicolored lights as she laughed and spun effortlessly in the arms of a male friend. Her carefree smile radiated warmth and ease, and the way her hair shimmered under the strobe lights made her seem almost untouchable—a dazzling creature from a world so far removed from Viktor's own that it might as well have been a fragment of some distant, elusive dream.

As midnight arrived, the atmosphere grew rowdier and more liberated. Several members of the group were visibly intoxicated, their laughter louder, voices carrying across the room, their movements looser and less restrained. One young man, barely able to maintain his balance, reached out and pulled Jelena back onto the dance floor. Viktor, stationed nearby and half-engaged in a muted conversation with one of the identical twins from Ascot, couldn't help but keep his gaze fixed on Jelena. She laughed freely, swaying rhythmically to the music with a natural, effortless grace. For a fleeting moment, Viktor felt a pang of something he didn't want to name—envy, longing, or perhaps a confusing mixture of both. The complexity of his feelings unsettled him, stirring questions about what Jelena truly meant to him, and whether that feeling was something deeper than mere obligation or protection.

The twin beside him continued speaking with animated gestures, her rapid, fluent English washing over Viktor like a persistent static hum. He nodded occasionally out of politeness, though the stream of words passed through him with little meaning. His mind remained elsewhere, tangled in thoughts he couldn't shake. Finally, sensing his lack of engagement, she reached out, grabbing his arm with an exasperated yet amused smile.

"Do you dance?" she asked, her tone teasing but with an unmistakable insistence.

Viktor nodded mutely, allowing himself to be gently led onto the crowded dance floor. The music thumped louder here, its deep bass vibrations echoing through his chest and stirring a restless energy beneath his skin. Around him, young partygoers moved with wild abandon—laughing, spinning, their bodies alive with uninhibited joy—a vivid contrast to Viktor's own tightly controlled, measured presence. At first, his movements were stiff and cautious, each step deliberate as he fought to match the rhythm without losing his footing. But the twin seemed effortlessly in her element, twirling and swaying beside him with the natural grace of someone born to these exuberant nights.

By 2 a.m., a suggestion arose to continue the party at a private residence. Viktor followed along reluctantly, his focus never straying far from Jelena, whose safety remained his paramount concern.

The apartment on Sloane Street was a sprawling testament to wealth and extravagance, every inch a sleek, modern masterpiece. The rooms were filled with minimalist yet luxurious furniture, and the walls were adorned with bold abstract art pieces that spoke of both status and artistic taste. Viktor's eyes scanned the space with a mixture of awe and disbelief, struggling to fathom how anyone could inhabit such excessive opulence as an everyday reality.

Taking a seat in the expansive living room, Viktor nursed a non-alcoholic drink, trying to maintain a semblance of detachment. His sense of discomfort grew as his gaze fell on the coffee table, where small mirrors lay arranged neatly, each dusted with precise lines of white powder. Around him, the partygoers seemed utterly oblivious to his unease, their laughter growing louder and more raucous as drinks and various substances flowed freely, dissolving inhibitions and blurring realities.

Viktor's eyes searched the room, finally settling on Jelena. She sat a few feet away, deeply engrossed in conversation with the young man she had danced with earlier. Relief washed over him to see that she hadn't touched the cocaine, but the way she leaned into the man's words, her hand occasionally brushing his arm in a casual, intimate gesture, sent a strange tightening sensation through Viktor's chest. He told himself it was merely concern for her safety, a professional instinct to shield her from potential danger. Yet deep down, he wasn't so sure. The feeling twisted into something more complex—an unsettling mix of protectiveness, jealousy, and a vague, unspoken worry about what he truly meant to her, and what she meant to him.

"Viktor?" Her voice cut sharply through the fog of his wandering thoughts, drawing his attention back with surprising clarity. She waved him over, her eyes bright and shimmering—whether from genuine excitement or the lingering effects of the evening's indulgences, he couldn't say. As he approached, she swayed slightly, steadying herself by resting a hand lightly on his arm.

"I don't think you've met my boyfriend," she said with a playful lilt in her voice, gently tugging at the collar of the man standing beside her.

The young man, who had just been bent over the coffee table moments before, straightened abruptly after inhaling a thin line of cocaine. His pupils were dilated, and his wavering gaze fixated on Viktor with unsteady focus. He offered a sloppy, uneven smile that didn't quite reach his eyes.

[160]

"Hey there," he slurred lazily. "John." He extended a clammy hand, which Viktor accepted with reluctance, shaking it firmly but without warmth.

"And you are?" John asked, though his attention wavered as Jelena leaned in close to whisper something inaudible into his ear.

"Oh yeah," John said with a lazy grin, clearly recalling something. "I remember you from the races. You're Jelena's bodyguard."

Before Viktor could respond, John was abruptly yanked away by another girl from the party, leaving Jelena standing awkwardly beside him. She watched John dance with her friend across the room, her expression carefully unreadable—neither entirely pleased nor upset, but somewhere in between.

"Are you having fun?" she asked softly, turning back toward Viktor with a brightness that felt more forced than genuine.

Viktor nodded, choosing his words carefully. "Yes. And you?"

"Fantastic," she replied with a faint, almost shy laugh. Then, without hesitation, she reached out and grabbed his hand. Her touch sent an unexpected jolt through him—a spark that tightened in his chest and made him pause for a fleeting moment.

But as she gently led him toward the makeshift dance floor, the music swelling around them, Viktor realized something unmistakable: in this moment, surrounded by the dizzying excess of a world he barely understood, he was willing to follow her anywhere. The night, the lights, the chaos—they all faded into the background as he stepped forward beside her, caught in the gravity of their shared connection.

Outside, the first light of dawn began to seep softly through the apartment windows, painting the room in gentle hues of pale pink and gold. The long night had slowly surrendered to the approaching morning. Some of the partygoers had already slipped away quietly, leaving the luxurious space in a gradual state of calm, while others were sprawled across couches, chairs, and corners of the sprawling apartment, deeply asleep in disheveled comfort.

Viktor and Jelena had danced for what felt like hours, the music and their shared moments blending into a gentle, glowing haze of connection and deepening intimacy. When finally they settled into seats near a vast window that offered a glimpse of the waking city beyond, Viktor felt a strange, soothing ease settle over him in her presence. It was as though the clamor of the night, the glittering chaos around them, had all faded into irrelevance, leaving only a fragile bubble of quiet and understanding between the two of them.

For a time, they spoke quietly, their voices low and steady, weaving gently into the muted buzz of the few remaining guests still awake elsewhere in the apartment.

"You dance better than I expected," Jelena teased, a faint smile playing at the corners of her lips, her eyes sparkling with warmth and something tender.

Viktor chuckled softly, scratching the back of his neck awkwardly. "Years of avoiding stepping on toes have finally paid off," he replied, a hint of self-deprecating humor in his voice.

She laughed quietly, leaning her elbow casually on the armrest beside her. "You don't talk much, do you?" she observed, her tone light but curious.

"Not when I don't have to," Viktor responded, his lips curving into a faint, genuine grin. "But I listen. That's something."

Jelena tilted her head slightly, studying him with an intensity that both unnerved and intrigued him. "And what have you heard tonight, then?"

He hesitated, his gaze locking briefly with hers, searching for the right words. "That you're… different from the others. In a good way."

Her cheeks flushed a delicate shade of pink, and she glanced down at the nearly empty champagne glass cradled in her hands. Just as she seemed about to respond, the expression on her face shifted; her eyes scanned the room, her brow furrowing with a flicker of concern.

"Have you seen John?" she asked softly, her voice tinged with curiosity and a subtle undercurrent of unease.

The intimate spell they'd shared shattered in that moment. Viktor hesitated before shaking his head slowly, his eyes following her as she rose and disappeared into the depths of the apartment in search of the young man.

Left alone, Viktor slumped deeper into his seat, fatigue pressing down on him like a heavy cloak. The exhaustion of the night finally caught up with him, his eyelids fluttering dangerously close to closure as he fought to remain alert. Minutes slipped by in a slow, oppressive crawl. He checked his watch again—fifteen minutes had passed. Where was she? The question lingered, heavy and unanswered, as the morning light continued to grow steadily outside.

A knot of unease twisted relentlessly in Viktor's stomach, an uncomfortable tightening that seemed to grow with each passing second. He rose abruptly from his seat, the exhaustion that had weighed heavily on him suddenly eclipsed by a rising tide of dread and urgency. Without hesitation, he began to move through the dimly lit apartment, stepping carefully past the sleeping forms of strangers sprawled across couches, chairs, and floors alike. His thoughts raced uncontrollably. I shouldn't have let her go alone, the silent reprimand echoed in his mind. Yet even as guilt gnawed at him, he tugged at the fragile thread of reassurance. She's still in the apartment. What could possibly happen here?

He pushed the thought aside and pressed on, his eyes scanning every shadowed corner until, at last, he found himself standing before one of the bathroom doors. The door was locked, but his firm knock prompted a faint shuffle from inside. After an anxious moment, the lock clicked, and Jelena slowly opened the door.

Her face was a haunting portrait of heartbreak. Her eyes, rimmed with raw red, brimmed with fresh tears that had streaked dark trails of mascara down her pale cheeks. She looked so small, so fragile, as if the weight of the entire world had suddenly descended upon her slender shoulders. It was as though time had paused, capturing the depth of her pain in that frozen instant.

"John…" Her voice trembled, barely more than a whisper. "He cheated on me," she choked out, the words thick with anguish and disbelief. "I found him in bed with another girl!" The confession spilled from her lips in ragged gasps, her voice cracking as she collapsed into uncontrollable sobs.

A sharp pang twisted deep in Viktor's chest at the sight of her suffering. Without a second thought, he stepped forward and closed the space between them, wrapping his arms carefully around her trembling frame. Her body shook against his, wracked with sobs that seemed to flow from a place deep within her soul. Gently, he stroked her back—his touch both firm and tender—as if trying to shield her from the searing pain, offering what little comfort he could.

"Why would he do this?" Jelena whispered, her voice muffled against his chest, fragile and broken. "I thought he cared…"

Viktor clenched his jaw tightly, anger flashing fiercely in his eyes—not directed at Jelena, but at the man who had brought her to this moment of devastation. "He's an idiot," Viktor said quietly, each word weighted with conviction. "Anyone who would hurt you doesn't deserve you."

She pulled back just slightly, searching his face with tear-filled eyes, vulnerability etched in every line. "Do you really mean that?" she asked softly, her voice nearly fragile enough to shatter.

[165]

He nodded without hesitation, his voice steady and sure. "I do."

As her sobs gradually faded into soft, broken breaths, Viktor's gaze fell to her tear-streaked face. The raw vulnerability she wore like a second skin tugged relentlessly at something deep inside him. Without thinking, without planning, he leaned in and pressed a gentle, tentative kiss to her cheek.

For a fleeting moment, the rest of the world—the party, the night, the risks and dangers looming around them—all melted away. In that fragile, fleeting connection, nothing else mattered but the shared warmth of two souls finding solace in each other's presence.